THE ASYLUM

DEBRA MELLER

Print ISBN 978-1-913419-84-4

I would like to dedicate this book to my son Brian, who will always be forever young.

PROLOGUE

Nothing about this place was familiar; not the room, nor the constant noise that filled the hallways with echoes of despair. Patty struggled to remember how she got there as fear and anxiety filled her head with all kinds of different scenarios, each one much worse than the last.

The lighting above her was very bright, and she could hardly make out the man's face that was standing over her. She could see that his lips were moving, but she couldn't understand a word he was saying. Patty tried to push his hands away as he was placing the electrodes to her temples, but her hands were tied down beside her. Suddenly, she felt a surge of electricity enter her body. Pain exploded in every fibre of her being as her body arched and soon after, she began to convulse. Everything went dark and when she finally awoke, several hours later, she had no concept of time or place. As she lay in an unfamiliar bed, desperately trying to remove her hands from the restraints, she prayed she would wake up from this nightmare.

Sometime later, maybe days, she found herself back in the room that she shared with three other strangers. Patty tried to focus on her surroundings and figure out who these people were, but no one seemed familiar. Right across from her was a frail old woman, sitting on the edge of her bed, picking scabs off her skin. The old woman smiled at Patty as she continued picking at her skin until it bled. The two other women in her room were screaming at each other, they were fighting over an old blanket that they both claimed ownership of. Down the hall, Patty could hear someone else screaming. The sounds were now so overwhelming and frightening that she put her pillow over her head to drown them out.

After a while, Patty tried to get out of bed to use the chamber pot that sat in the corner of the room. A torn curtain draped around it did nothing to give anyone privacy. As much as she tried to stand, her legs wouldn't carry her, and she fell back into her bed. Patty had no recollection of being paralyzed from the waist down two years earlier. It was as if this painful time in her life had been completely erased from her memory.

Feeling frightened, she called out, "Help me, someone please help me!"

The elderly woman picking at her skin began rocking back and forth as she laughed hysterically. A few minutes later, one of the women that was fighting over the blanket came over to Patty's bed and yanked her blanket off her.

As she stood over Patty, she shouted, "If you take my blanket again, you'll be sorry!"

Patty tried to call for help but her voice was weak and frail. As she lay on her bed, covered only in a dirty cotton hospital gown, she tried to make sense of what was happening to her. Feeling helpless and vulnerable she began to cry and still no one seemed to notice she was there. Unable to feel her bladder release its contents, she now lay in her own urine.

Patty turned to see that the two women that were previously fighting over a dirty blanket were now content as they sat quietly chatting. The old woman continued to pick at her arms and face, but thankfully she had stopped laughing. As the sun came through the only window in the tiny room, it revealed the appalling conditions that surrounded her. Rat faeces were scattered about and the walls were damp with mould in every corner of the room. Dried blood and bodily fluids made the old wooden floor an ideal place for bacteria to thrive. Wherever she was, it was not a place for the faint of heart.

Unsure what time or even what day it was, Patty became startled when the sound of bells began to ring throughout. She had no idea that this horrendously loud noise, was a call to the patients to come to the dining room. Her roommates seemed programmed as all three immediately stopped what they were doing and left the room. Soon the noise stopped, and Patty remained still; all she could hope for was that someone would come and take her home. Patty had been overlooked again. As she lay in her filthy bed, she looked up at the cracked and broken plaster on the ceiling above her. She was malnourished and weak and despite feeling cold and uncomfortable, she soon fell back to sleep. This was Patty's only escape, but sadly, her nightmare had just begun.

1

I t was the summer of 1907 and Amelia Fern had been dead for almost two months. She had been looking after Patty's every need since helping to deliver her son, Ian. Amelia had been a brilliant midwife and a wonderful caregiver and because of Patty's paralysis, she had been the obvious choice when it came to delivering her baby. Patty relied on Amelia for everything since her husband, Chris, had virtually given up on his wife following the accident that had caused her to lose the use of her legs. But sadly, Amelia began to experience some psychosis and had even come to believe that Patty was her own daughter. This had come about suddenly and without warning. When Amelia left Patty's home to get supplies on a cold winter's day in February, she'd had every intention to return. If not for an undiagnosed heart condition, she would have. In April of that same year, Amelia would pass away after spending almost three months in the hospital. Unfortunately, without Amelia in her life, Patty's life and the life of her infant son would be put in jeopardy.

On that fateful day, Amelia had been travelling on foot for many miles when she became disoriented. Snow had blanketed much of the rural area where she lived, and after walking in circles for several hours she began to feel weak and short of breath. If not for the help of strangers, Amelia would have died that day, and chances are her body wouldn't have been recovered until the spring. When she finally arrived at Orillia's Memorial Hospital, she was barely alive, having suffered a near-fatal heart attack and spending several hours outdoors in freezing temperatures. After being stabilized physically which took several weeks, her physician referred her to psychiatry when he noticed she had no memory of what had happened to her and limited cognitive abilities. Doctor Shaw was a dedicated psychiatrist and over the months had tried to gain her trust and diagnose her mental illness. Just prior to her death, Amelia did regain most of her memories and she left a personal journal behind for the doctor. Although the writing was illegible at times, Doctor Shaw was able to piece together the puzzle that was Amelia's life and would eventually answer many of his questions and tell him why she had suffered an emotional breakdown.

Doctor Shaw was the head of psychiatry at the hospital and had written many articles on the subject. During his time with Amelia he had learned that despite her physical decline, she was extremely intelligent and had been a practising midwife for many years. He was intrigued by her inner strength and he took his time as he helped her to recall her past. During her stay at the hospital she was diagnosed with psychosis as well as congestive heart failure. It had taken quite a while before Amelia began to trust him. In the beginning she had insisted she was the mother of two infant children, a daughter, Charity, and a son, Ian, but Amelia was sixty-four years old and the doctor knew it was impossible for her to have such a young family.

Throughout his time with her he was able to surmise that Charity had been born to one of the mothers Amelia had cared for and had been born with many birth defects that were not detected right away. Her death had been the turning point in Amelia's life. She had felt responsible, although no one else had felt this way, and eventually her guilt had consumed her. In the last ten pages of her journal, she began writing notes that told a story about a man named William Blows, his wife Elise and their maid Mavis. Amelia had confessed to poisoning Mr. Blows and she listed the reasons why she had done this, some of which were very disturbing, including his brutality and complete disregard for his wife and child's well-being.

Amelia also mentioned her own daughter Lila, who was married. And she went into great detail about a woman called Patty Miller and her husband Chris. She referred to Chris as an "evil man" who flaunted his mistresses in front of Patty. She told of Patty's paralysis and the difficulty she'd had delivering her son, Ian. She didn't mention where Patty lived or how to contact her family and friends.

From Amelia's notes, Dr Shaw learned how passionate she was about women's rights and how she felt when these rights were neglected. Amelia left behind many questions, but Doctor Shaw was satisfied she had been at peace when she died. He had eventually been able to locate Elise Blows and informed her and her daughter of Amelia's death. Devastated at the news, the two women made a special trip to London, Ontario, to give Amelia's daughter, Lila, the dreadful news. Lila, as expected, was heartbroken; her mother had never met her only grandchild, Isabel Anne, who was now three and a half months old. Amelia had been so consumed with Patty Miller's well-being that she had neglected her own family. Lila immediately made up her mind to go back to Elmvale with Elise and Mavis as she had the emotionally draining task of arranging her mother's funeral. Amelia would be laid to rest alongside her husband in Sunset Gardens. It was only after her death that Lila, Elise and Mavis learned about Amelia's mental breakdown. No one knew that her mind had become unsettled after the loss of Elise's daughter, Charity, and that she had blamed herself for this little girl's tragic death.

All three women felt very guilty for not being there for Amelia when she was alive. Elise took to her bed for a week afterwards. She was indebted to Amelia for what she had done and felt responsible for not recognizing that her closest friend was spiralling downwards. After a quiet ceremony and a few short days with Elise and Mavis, Lila returned home. A memorial to celebrate Amelia's life would take place in June of that same year, this was something Lila knew her mother would approve of. Lila returned to London devastated as she now had to come to terms with losing her mother. In order to keep her mind busy, she spent the next few months arranging the memorial.

Amelia had birthed many babies in her years as a practising midwife and was highly respected in the community, and Lila made a point of inviting everyone that had been touched by her mother. A celebration of her life was perfect for someone who had brought so many lives into this world. By the time the memorial began there was standing room only in the church, and it had been a wonderful afternoon as several women told their story about the time Amelia had delivered their children. Some had broken down in tears as they talked about Amelia's willingness to help, even if they had been unable to pay for her services.

When it came to Elise's turn to talk about her dear friend, she began to sob. She told the guests, "Many would have let my Charity die, but Amelia insisted she had the same right to life as every other infant she delivered. If it weren't for Amelia's bravery and devotion, I know I would be in a much darker place. Amelia was the light that took me away from the darkness that had enveloped me, she was much more than a friend and l will never forget her."

Although most people in town knew about little Charity, no one knew the truth behind her husband's untimely death. For Elise and Mavis, Amelia had been a godsend and neither one would ever forget the sacrifices she made for them.

During Lila's stay in Elmvale, where her mother had lived and worked, Elise and Mavis both noticed how she took after her mother. Like her mother before her, Lila had begun to deliver babies, and she had also joined the suffragette movement and was now deeply involved in women's rights, including their right to vote. She also told Elise and Mavis about the suffering of women at the hands of their husbands. She specifically mentioned a young mother named Julian Wonch, who had recently given birth to her twelfth child. Julian was only twenty-nine years old and her first baby had been born when she was just fourteen. She said Julian's husband was a wicked man, much like Elise's husband had been.

"Can you imagine, he demanded Julian do her wifely duties even though she had not healed from birthing her child?"

Elise knew exactly what that felt like, but she also knew Lila had no idea of what she had gone through or how Amelia had helped to end her suffering. Elise was very proud of Lila, who now seemed to take over from where her own mother had left off; fighting to bring women out of the dark ages.

After the ceremony that evening, Lila asked about Patty Miller. She wondered if either Elise or Mavis knew how she was. Sadly, they had been so devastated by Amelia's death that they had completely forgotten about Patty. Lila knew her mother would never forgive her if she didn't check up on her, and she knew she couldn't leave town without finding out if the woman was okay.

She told Elise and Mavis, "I owe it to my mother to make

sure Patty has been cared for, I know how much my mother loved that child."

Both Mavis and Elise agreed, none of what had happened to Amelia was Patty's fault. Lila decided to make a visit to Patty's home, but unfortunately she would not find Patty there.

2

It had been two days since Patty was brought back from the infirmary, and she was still lying in her own excrement, hoping someone would come by and take her out of this place. Patty shut her eyes and covered her ears with her hands as she tried to block out the constant screaming. She felt so cold, but no one was around to help her. Just as she thought things couldn't get much worse, she was startled by someone pulling at her arms. When she opened her eyes she saw a large man in a white coat, and he pulled her arms so hard, she felt one of them come out of its socket. The pain was unbearable and she began to scream, but screaming was constant there and it came from all directions, so no one bothered to check on her.

The man ignored her cries and continued pulling at her arms. "Get up!" he shouted.

Patty replied, "I can't get up; can't you see something has happened to my legs?"

Just then, another man who looked unkempt came into the room, he whispered something to the larger man trying to get Patty up, then he left. A few minutes later he came back with a chair with wheels and pushed it toward Patty's bed. Patty felt vulnerable as she desperately tried to conceal herself. The filthy cotton gown she had been wearing for days was now pushed up so high it exposed her breasts. The two men took turns groping her. Patty tried to push them away, but one of her arms was hanging limp by her side and the other was so thin and weak she just didn't have the strength. Patty was helpless and unable to stop them, until finally someone heard her calls for help.

Nurse Fiona just happened to be on that floor and came rushing into Patty's room. The minute she realized what was going on, she shouted, "Get your filthy hands off her!"

She then pushed the men aside and warned them that she would be speaking to someone in charge before she finished her shift that day. By this time Patty was trembling as tears rolled down her cheeks. As the nurse raised Patty into a sitting position, she noticed her arm dangling precariously below the shoulder.

She then told Patty to shut her eyes for a moment, and with one hard push and a slight twist she popped her injured arm back into place. As painful as this was, surprisingly, Patty did not flinch once.

Nurse Fiona was a gentle giant, standing taller than most of her male counterparts. She explained to Patty that she had missed the dinner bell and now would have to wait until four o'clock for her tea. She told her she would come by just before and prepare her.

When Patty asked like she had many times before, "Where am l, why am I here?" Nurse Fiona had smiled and said, "Oh, Patty, l have told you every day since you arrived months ago. You are in the Hillside Asylum, don't you remember?"

"Why, how did l get here?"

But Nurse Fiona just shook her head knowingly, then gently covered Patty up before leaving the room.

Patty had been in Hillside since February but she had no

recollection of where she had been prior to this. Her overall condition when she arrived had been dreadful; her body emaciated and she had been covered in lice. On arrival she was taken straight to the infirmary and given a bath in kerosene. Finally, after days spent in relative darkness with only the occasional visit from a doctor, she was transferred to the baths in the cellar and washed from head to toe in lye soap. Only after this was considered successful in removing the remaining head lice was she assigned to her room. Still weak and malnourished, she remained in a relatively unstable condition that continued to this day.

Shortly after Nurse Fiona left the room, the elderly woman returned and sat on Patty's bed, picking at her facial scabs. Although her face looked familiar, Patty didn't remember where she had seen her before. Although she had seen her roommates every day since she arrived, each day was completely new to her and very frightening. The elderly woman was called Lois Russel and she was seventy-three years old. Lois had been a resident of Hillside Asylum since 1901 after murdering a shopkeeper for not giving her the correct change. She had received shock treatments and took a long list of medications and was considered a danger to others, although she was not isolated from the rest of the population.

The two other women Patty shared with were twin sisters, Rebecca and Adeline, both aged twenty-one. Rebecca and Adeline had been abandoned by their parents when they were six months old and had spent their entire life with strangers. First as residents at the Oak Park Orphanage and later with adoptive parents. But when they could no longer afford to keep them, they had been dropped off at the asylum at the age of ten. Neither one had any history of mental health issues, but Rebecca had developed some anger issues and was given a rather rudimentary lobotomy, leaving her temperament much worse than it had ever been. Adeline was wrongly diagnosed as being depressed and had received shock treatments over a two-year period. Now, after spending eleven years at Hillside, they had become institutionalized and could no longer function outside the walls of the asylum.

When Patty Miller was admitted to the asylum, she had been catatonic. She did not speak or appear to understand what was spoken to her. Her vital signs were unstable and she was extremely dehydrated. A few weeks later, she began asking anyone who would listen if they knew why she was there. In some ways this was a godsend. Thankfully, she did not recall anything about her time prior to being admitted, and she didn't know what had happened to her or her infant son. She was later diagnosed with acute hysteria and psychosis. Her overall prognosis was grim and unless there was an intervention, Patty Miller would probably spend the rest of her life in conditions that were not fit for human habitation.

3

Back in Elmvale, Lila was true to her word and early the next morning she made her way to Chris and Patty Miller's farm. It seemed strange going there now, as Lila was heading back to a place where her mother had begun to lose her grip on reality. Still, it was something she felt she had to do, but now, Lila wasn't certain what she would find as her mother had once told her about Patty's physical limitations, and she knew that she was a vulnerable young woman who lived with a man that cared very little about her.

As soon as Lila arrived at the entrance to the property, she was met by two large dogs. Before she could secure her horse, they began barking and growling aggressively, which caused her horse to buck several times and nearly ended with her falling to the ground. She had never been a fan of large dogs after being bitten by one when she was a child.

A few minutes later, as Lila stood outside the locked gate, afraid to enter, an unfamiliar middle-aged woman came walking towards her. Lila shouted, "Excuse me, Miss, does Patty Miller still live here?" The woman didn't answer, but kept coming towards her. As she got closer to the gate, she ordered the dogs to go and Lila watched them retreat towards the house. The woman then introduced herself as Nelly Harthstone and asked Lila if she would like to come inside for a cool drink.

Lila followed her and tied her horse, Billy, to the fence that ran along the entire perimeter of the property, whilst Nelly locked the dogs inside the barn adjacent to the house. Billy was a very powerful horse and could be unpredictable at times, but now that the dogs were out of sight, he began to relax. Lila had been riding since she was just six years old, but Mavis had warned her that Billy didn't like other animals and often became extremely nervous around them.

The minute she was inside the old house, it was very apparent that Patty and Chris no longer lived there. When Lila had visited the house when her mother was staying there it had been run-down and had appeared dingy and unkept. Dirty clothes and piles of old farm equipment had been scattered inside and out. She also recalled that there had been an over-whelming smell of urine, and she had tried not to react to it when she had first met Patty, who had been incontinent since her accident. Lila knew that her husband did little to keep his wife or the bed linens clean that she soiled each night. When Amelia had first come into Patty's life her buttocks had been red, covered in blisters and she'd had several open sores on her coccyx. Lila knew now that if it wasn't for her mother's care Patty would have eventually died from infection.

But now the house resembled the beauty that surrounded it. It was immaculate and the dirty film that covered the windows was gone, allowing the sun to shine through and illuminate the beautiful hardwood floors. Nelly told Lila that she and her husband had worked day and night to restore it back to its orig-inal state. The whole interior had changed, and the smell of urine was no longer in the air, instead it was replaced by the lemon oil that they used to clean the floors. Fresh flowers adorned the oak mantelpiece that was once covered in dust and debris.

Once they were sitting down in the parlour, Nelly asked, "Now, young lady, how can I help you?"

Lila, like her mother, Amelia, always got to the point and quickly replied, "Do you know where I can find the previous owners, Chris and Patty Miller?" As soon as she asked the question, Nelly's facial expression changed. It was as if Lila had been the only person living within a ten-mile radius of the Miller farm who didn't know what had taken place there.

Before answering, Nelly asked Lila, "Are you a relative of the Millers?"

Lila said no, then explained that her mother had been Patty's caretaker before she herself had become ill. She added, "Patty and my mother were inseparable for a time, as my mother tended to her every need."

Nelly sat back, as though unsure if she should be telling this stranger the dreadful story about Patty and her infant son, Ian. Lila knew that something wasn't right as an uncomfortable silence settled around them for a few minutes. Nelly didn't say a thing as she got up and went into her husband's library. When she returned, she was holding newspaper clippings.

Nelly wondered why Lila hadn't heard what had gone on in the home, considering she had mentioned that her mother had been Patty's caretaker, and as a Christian woman she hated gossip, so before showing her the clippings, she asked if she read the *Elmvale Examiner*.

Lila smiled and said, "I used too, mother always insisted I read it each week to keep up on current events, but when I moved to London I began reading their local paper."

Nelly now understood why she hadn't seen the story and felt comfortable telling Lila what had happened.

"When we first moved in here the reporters hounded us day

and night. For a moment, when I saw you out there, l must confess that I thought you were one of them."

Lila was confused, she had no idea what Nelly was talking about, but then Nelly moved the paper towards her, and as Lila glanced down, she noticed the headline in big bold letters.

PATTY MILLER FOUND UNCONSCIOUS HOLDING HER DECEASED INFANT SON.

The date was February 27, 1907. Nelly could see the headlines had upset Lila and reached out to take her hand. Lila had no idea this had happened and when she saw the heartbreaking photo of Patty's infant son being taken from the home, she could no longer hold herself together. Tears came flooding down her face, and she couldn't help but think of her own small child. Lila wondered why Elise and Mavis hadn't mentioned anything about this, surely the tragic news about baby Miller would have spread through the town very quickly?

Nelly said the paper had printed several stories about Patty and Chris Miller, but some of the articles she read just sensationalized what really happened. She told Lila it was the bank manager who had found poor Patty after not being able to locate Chris Miller regarding the sale of his home.

"Since Mr. Briggs discovered the gruesome sight, he has not been able to return to work."

The story was heartbreaking and the more Lila learned, the worse it became. According to Patty's husband Chris, it had been a tragic accident and he did not take any responsibility for the death of his son or the condition of his wife.

In reality, Chris Miller had abandoned his wife and son, leaving Patty alone without nourishment or even enough coal to heat her home.

Nelly explained what she had been told. "According to the bank manager, Chris Miller had a mistress called Casandra Adams who lived on Christian Island, several miles north of

Elmvale." She paused, then continued. "Chris was so taken by her beauty, he abandoned his duties as a husband and father and left Patty entirely alone sometime in February, with just enough coal to last a few days.

"According to Mr. Briggs there wasn't a drop of food or even a ounce of milk in the home. Patty was near death when he found her sitting by the window in the parlour, still cradling her infant son. Unsure how she managed to get into a chair, Mr. Briggs assumed that this was where her husband had left her before heading to Christian Island to be with his mistress."

Lila asked, "What happened to Patty? Is she alive, did she make a full recovery?"

"I believe she was taken to the hospital, then transferred to a sanatorium. Some said she had completely lost her mind."

It was a heartbreaking story and to make matters worse, Nelly told Lila that Chris Miller was eventually charged with abandoning his wife and child, but never spent a day in jail.

Lila was infuriated, this was just another example of how men who neglected their wives seemed to walk away unscathed. She had been working vigilantly trying to inform and educate women on their rights. She also handed out pamphlets to let women know that they did have options and places to go if they were being abused in any way. This despicable act just confirmed her deepest fears; women in the eyes of their husbands and the law were seen as second-class citizens. She just couldn't understand why Chris Miller was not in prison, his actions directly caused the death of his infant son and the mental breakdown of his wife.

Nelly agreed with Lila. "Until the courts accept women as equal to men, nothing will ever change." She told Lila, "After hearing Patty's story my husband and I had second thoughts about purchasing this home; I was sure it wasn't for us, but my husband couldn't pass up a good deal."

Lila knew that if it were up to her, the house would have been torn down, but she couldn't share those views with Nelly. To Lila, the house was such a sad reminder of her own mother's demise and the death of an innocent child. After Lila thanked Nelly for her hospitality, she headed back to find out why Elise and Mavis had not known about the tragic events that had taken place there.

On the way back, she couldn't help but wonder what had happened to Patty and if she was still alive. She knew that if her mother was still here her heart would be broken to hear the tragic story and Lila promised there and then that she wouldn't rest until Patty was found. Patty deserved justice and someone needed to speak on her behalf. As Lila rode past her mother's home on her way to Elise's, she stopped for a moment. So much had changed in such a short time. Just sitting on her horse looking up at the bedroom she slept in as a child brought tears to her eyes. If only she had known that her mother was ill, if only she had come back home. The guilt she felt was over-whelming, and now she had to live knowing that her mother had died surrounded by strangers.

As she sat contemplating how things would have been if she had remained in Elmvale, for a moment she swore she could see her mother peeking out at her from the parlour window. Amelia had often done this as she had waited for Lila to return from school. Seconds later, the image was gone, and her sadness returned, but as she continued on her way that afternoon, she was sure she could still smell her mother's perfume in the air around her.

It was late afternoon when she got back to Elise's home. The children were napping and the home felt eerily quiet. Lila had not even sat down before she asked Elise and Mavis why they hadn't told her about the tragic events that had taken place in Patty's home. Both were completely unaware that this had happened and only when Mavis thought back to that time, did she suddenly remember that for the month of February, the entire family had been stricken with flu. Doctor Hammond had insisted they stay inside to avoid passing it on to someone else as influenza had already taken several lives.

"We were so ill that we had not even attended one church service that month."

Lila had had no idea they had been ill; she had written to both Elise and Mavis at that time and now she knew why they hadn't responded. Both women felt extremely sad for Patty, and wondered if they had known about Amelia's condition at the time if they could have done something to possibly change the outcome.

With so many unanswered questions, Lila thought her head would explode. All she could think about was the anger she had felt towards her mother at the time. Amelia had become so focused on Patty's care, that she had slowly began to separate herself from her own daughter and two closest friends. All along, Lila had thought that her mother had been pushing her away, punishing her for moving to London and leaving her in Elmvale alone. But Lila had never, ever considered that her mother was having a mental breakdown. No one had any idea that Amelia was so ill and now it was too late to help her.

Lila rested later that afternoon for about an hour but didn't sleep. She was so angry at Chris Miller for abandoning his crippled wife and infant son that she had told Elise and Mavis, "I will not rest until this scoundrel is behind bars for what he has done!" Lila also mentioned her determination to find out what had happened to Patty since the newspapers had stopped keeping track of her and no one was really sure where she'd ended up.

Neither Mavis nor Elise attempted to talk her out of it. They

knew that she was just like her mother, strong-willed and determined, and that she had already made her mind made up.

Instead, Mavis asked, "How can we help? We owe your
mother a great debt, because without her neither of us would
have survived William's abuse."

Although this statement was odd, when Lila asked what
Mavis meant by it, she immediately changed the subject.
Knowing it was best not to press Mavis for answers, she let it go.
Lila 's main concern at that moment was to convince her
husband, Isaac, that she needed to stay in Elmvale for an
extended period of time. Isaac was generally very understanding, but sometimes he disagreed with his wife's outrageous
behaviour.

Just before she had given birth to their daughter, Lila had
been arrested for protesting in front of the mayor's home in
London. Lila, along with several other women, had formed a
human chain and would not allow the mayor or his family in or
out of their home. The women insisted that the mayor was
receiving money from the owner of a seedy beer parlour. Their
accusations of inhumane treatment of their female staff had
caused an uproar in London and eventually the establishment
had closed its doors for good. But Isaac had been furious when
he'd had to come to the constabulary and bail his pregnant wife
out. After that incident, Isaac had begun setting ground rules
that he expected Lila to follow.

However, Isaac had soon learned that Lila did as she pleased
and would continue to do so. He often referred to his wife as
being pig-headed and stubborn, but despite what he felt were
her shortcomings, he was still deeply in love with her.

Elise and Mavis gave Lila some privacy as she spoke to Isaac
about staying in Elmvale. Although they tried not to listen to
what they were saying, they couldn't help but hear some of Lila's
conversation. Her voice was normally soft and sweet, but they

could hear it becoming louder and more aggressive as she spoke to her husband. Lila insisted that she was staying in Elmvale for as long as it took to bring justice for Patty and her infant son. Isaac was clearly not pleased with his wife, and although they could not hear his side of the conversation, Lila's last words to him were, "No, I cannot save the world or put a time limit on this, you will have to get along without me!" Then Elise and Mavis heard the phone slam down. Lila's face was red when she came into the parlour, but neither of them commented on the phone call, and they both assured Lila that she and Isabel Anne could stay for as long as she wanted to.

With her mind made up, Lila wasn't going to waste any more time and now needed a plan of action. Nelly had mentioned that an editor at the *Elmvale Examiner* had followed the story closely and that he might know where Patty had ended up, or at the very least, where Chris Miller was living now. His description of Chris Miller made Lila believe that he too felt that this man had got away with murder. In one of the articles he had described Chris as a man with no morals and devoid of empathy. Lila was determined to find Patty and, if she could, reopen the neglect and abandonment case against her husband. Lila knew this wouldn't be easy and that she couldn't do it on her own. With this in mind, she decided to enlist the help of a close friend and fellow suffragette, Loraine Powel. Loraine was strong and determined and the head of the local chapter for the Sisters of the Suffragette movement in London, and Lila knew she could count on her. Loraine reminded Lila of her mother, a woman that would never turn her back on anyone, especially someone like Patty Miller who had lost everything.

4

P atty awoke to see Nurse Fiona standing over her and again she asked, "Where am l, what am l doing here?"

An imposing sight, Nurse Fiona was almost six feet tall with a strong, muscular build and had worked at Hillside Asylum since soon after she moved to Ancaster in the Spring of 1903. She lived alone with her three cats and spent her afternoons off volunteering at the local homeless shelter. Fiona had a reputation for being a soft touch when it came to the patients, but she was very strict with the attendants, especially if they did not follow the rules. Shortly after Patty had been accosted, the two male staff responsible had been dismissed.

This had little to do with her report of the incident to the man in charge of the asylum, Mr. Potter – he rarely listened to the nurses. No, this was down to a shareholder who had received a letter detailing what had happened. His wife had insisted that he withdraw his support if the two men weren't removed immediately. Rumours surrounding their dismissal told of an anonymous letter that had been sent to the shareholder and although Nurse Fiona denied sending it, she had mentioned that she had been put off by Mr. Potter's reluctance to get rid of these questionable individuals. A bright young woman, Nurse Fiona knew that if she pushed the owner too far, he could simply fire her. Sending the letter anonymously had been the perfect plan and it just happened to work.

Nurse Fiona couldn't help but feel sorry for Patty. Since being admitted to Hillside she had not had one visitor. As she lifted Patty into a wheelchair, she could feel her bones protruding through her gown, thin and fragile, and Nurse Fiona couldn't help but wonder how many meals she was missing. None of the staff paid much attention to this particular patient and she knew that it was very likely that Patty was doing without more often than not.

Although Nurse Fiona detested much of what was happening in the asylum, she knew that she was replaceable and she also knew her limitations. Mr. Potter didn't appreciate any sort of criticism about the home or the staff that worked there, and he thought nothing of firing anyone he felt might be a troublemaker.

The dining area was very dark, cold and uninviting. Long dirty tables lined the massive room and rats could be seen scattering as more and more patients filled the space. Patty pleaded with Nurse Fiona to take her back to her room, the noise and clattering of the pots and pans making her increasingly more anxious and frightened. The line-up for the food was excessive but the sparse kitchen staff tried their best to serve each and every patient. Nurse Fiona wheeled Patty into the line as she was too weak to wheel herself; her muscles had begun to atrophy, giving her little strength to do even the smallest tasks. Some of the more irrational patients screamed at the staff and flung their food everywhere.

A fight broke out between two patients in front of Patty and she cowered in fear. The women were fighting over the last potato, each one claiming it was theirs. This was not unusual as food had been rationed since Mr. Potter had purchased the facility. His only concern was saving money, and the more he could save the better. And since most of the patients rarely had a visitor, no one from outside of the facility ever noticed how lean the patients' meals had become.

As attendants attempted to break up the fight, Patty cowered in her chair. A few minutes later a loud male voice shouted, "Sit down and be quiet or we will remove those causing a disturbance and send them into the Preston Wing!"

The name sounded familiar to Patty, and she recalled a fleeting, disturbing memory of being in that wing, but she wasn't sure why. The minute the attendant threatened to take the women to the Preston Wing, the whole room went quiet and the people fighting continued down the line. As Patty pushed her tray along, the staff put a bowl of vegetable soup and a piece of bread on it. Patty continued to move along and was given a cup of tea and a sweet roll. Behind her someone shouted, "Get moving, lady, we don't have all day!"

Patty tried to balance the tray on her lap, but most of the tea and soup spilled onto the floor. By the time she got to a table she had very little to eat. Her bread was soggy from the fluid that had spilled and the little bit of leftover soup was now just broth. Patty began to cry as she was being pushed and shoved by the other patients sitting next to her. Nothing made any sense; who were all these people and how did she end up in such an awful place? Sadly, as much as she tried, she still could not remember how she had even got there.

A little while later, the bell rang three times and Patty watched as everyone got up and started walking towards the doors. Unsure what to do, she tried to follow the crowd, but her arms were too weak to wheel herself the entire way out. Within a few minutes the dining room was empty except for two of the kitchen staff. Unable to hold the heavy door open enough to get through, she became stuck between the door and the hallway. Patty called out for help, but as was always the way with the asylum staff, no one paid any attention to her. The servers cleared the tables but neither of them went to help Patty.

She could hear them clearly chattering in the background and called again, "Someone please take me home."

As the staff left the dining area through the side door, they shut off the lights, leaving Patty behind, frightened and confused. There wasn't a soul around and all she could hear were the rats scattering about. A few seconds later she felt something crawling on her left hand, one of the rats had tried reaching her lap to steal a piece of the uneaten sweet roll. Patty began screaming which startled the rodent who then nipped her hand before running off with the morsel of food. Finally, her screams were heard and the evening nurse came running down the hall wondering what all the noise was about.

Nurse Margaret Reid wasn't as comforting as Nurse Fiona was, and the moment she saw Patty she slapped her across the face and shouted, "Shut up or l will insist they send you back to the Preston Wing."

Nurse Margaret wheeled Patty back to her room and neglected to even notice the puncture wound or the blood on her frock that had been caused by the rodent's bite. Without tending to her needs, she quickly lifted Patty into bed and left the room. Rebecca and Adeline were standing by the window and they also ignored Patty as she cried out in pain.

Adeline was trying to wipe the filth off the window with her sleeve. She wanted to see if the rabbits had returned to nest under the old abandoned carriage at the side of the building. Lois was already in bed, she often slept most of the evening, then wandered the halls late at night, searching for her daughter, Rose, who had died many years ago. Shortly after her death, Lois began having paranoid delusions believing people were plotting to steal her money and burn down her home. Eight months after her daughter had died, she stabbed Mr. Carter, the proprietor of her local mercantile piercing his heart and causing him to die instantly. When she was found a few days later, she had taken the same knife she had used to kill him and poked numerous superficial holes in her face and arms.

The judge found that she was criminally insane and ordered her into the asylum for the remainder of her life. When she'd arrived, the wounds on her face were treated with a menthol paste but they never healed, Lois wouldn't let them and they were always oozing and infected and within a few months, the staff gave up treating them. A psychiatric doctor called John Lawlor surmised that she would never allow them to heal because she blamed herself for her daughter's death. By keeping the wounds open, she was punishing herself each and every day.

Despite the noise that evening and the screams that echoed throughout the building all through the night, Patty managed to fall into a fretful sleep. It was sometime before sunrise when she awoke, unable to catch her breath. Patty felt a heavy pressure on her face and chest then heard a familiar laugh and realized that Lois was holding a pillow over her face as she attempted to smother her. Patty used all her strength until finally she knocked Lois to the floor, causing her to hit her head on the iron railing. Lois screamed out in pain and Nurse Margaret, who was just about to end her shift, came rushing in. She took one look at Lois who was now bleeding profusely and demanded to know what had happened. Lois began laughing hysterically all the while trying to wipe the blood off her face and on to Nurse Margaret's clean white frock.

She then pointed to Patty and said, "She did it! She tried to kill me, now arrest her immediately."

Patty, who was so frightened by the incident, couldn't find the right words to explain what had happened. Nurse Margaret was now in a foul mood and immediately called for an orderly. Patty was then unceremoniously thrown onto a gurney and her hands were strapped to her side. Nurse Margaret told the attendant to take Patty to the Preston Wing and then tended to the cut on Lois's face. In her notes, Nurse Margaret wrote: *0600 hours Patty Miller purposely knocked Lois Russel to the ground for no apparent reason, causing grievous injury.*

Unbeknown to Patty, Lois's attempt to smother her and her reaction to this had sealed her fate. She would now have to endure several painful electric shock treatments. The Preston Wing was named after the doctor who had discovered electric shock treatment and the so-called benefits of isolation. He insisted that any patient that exhibited violent behaviour should be isolated from the rest and endure electric shock treatments until they deemed the person more compliant.

He felt that if done properly it could significantly alter the outcome of the mentally ill. He even wrote an article stating that one patient had been completely cured and released back into society only ten months after arriving with a diagnosis of manic hysteria with abusive tendencies. The problem was, there had never been a patient and Doctor Preston was eventually found to be a fraud. And yet his treatment continued even after his death in 1905. Most of the patients that received electric shock treatment struggled with more problems afterwards, including memory loss and tremors. He also recommended that these patients be isolated for several days. His was a treatment so radical that most asylums stopped doing this, but Hillside did not.

Some of the overworked and underpaid staff insisted their patients needed it, simply because afterwards they would become quiet and non-confrontational. This was the third time

Nurse Margaret had sent Patty to the Preston Wing. She never once considered Patty's frail condition and seemed to get some enjoyment out of frightening her and several others.

After Patty received her third electric shock therapy that night, she became unresponsive and was placed in an ice bath. This controversial treatment was performed by one of the resident psychiatrists, Doctor Frank Parsons, who insisted it would have lasting benefits. Patty was submerged into the bath and even after she began to come around she was held there by two assistants for almost a half hour. Her whole body shook as the freezing cold water crept up to her chin. Doctor Parsons noted that Patty immediately responded to the treatment which in turn made him feel justified for doing it in the first place. Most of the attendants felt it was a bit radical, but no one dared speak up. Sadly, Mr. Potter wasn't the kind of man that one could talk to freely and depending on his mood, you could be fired just by bringing this to his attention. Patty was then taken into a damp, dark room in the cellar for another full day. No one came in to see her during this time.

Patty fell in and out of consciousness during most of her time there. She had not had any nourishment in two and half days and the shock treatment had left her in such a state that she didn't have the strength to complain. She was eventually returned to her room where she slept for seventeen hours straight. It wasn't until Nurse Fiona returned from her three days off that she found Patty in a terrible state. Patty had developed a high fever, her left hand was terribly swollen and her coccyx had a large open bedsore so deep she could see the underlying tissue. As she reviewed Nurse Margaret's notes, Fiona saw that it was her who had insisted Patty was combative and had caused grievous injury to Lois Russel and had insisted she needed the shock treatment. Nurse Fiona also noted the electric shock treatment and subsequent ice bath.

Nurse Fiona was furious; she knew that Patty was incapable of injuring anyone. She then took a baster from the kitchen and filled it with a mixture of warm water and salt. After explaining what she was doing to Patty, she turned her on her side and squirted the warm mixture into her wound. Because Patty hadn't been properly cleaned in days, dried faeces had imbedded into the opening. Once Nurse Fiona was satisfied she had removed all of it, she put salve onto some clean gauze and placed it over the wound. Patty seemed to trust her and didn't flinch during the entire procedure. She then took Patty's left hand and put it into some cold water hoping to decrease the swelling. During her treatments Patty remained silent and just stared at the wall beside her bed. Her condition was very poor and the nurse had to summon Doctor Asher to her room. He was the assistant psychiatrist; a kinder, gentler version of Doctor Parsons. After Nurse Fiona explained how deep her coccyx wound was, he ordered a boric acid wash followed by a honey dressing. He saw that her hand was very swollen and noted the signs of a rodent bite. He took a scalpel out of his kit and quickly excised the wound causing its contents to spill out. A combination of blood and pus oozed from the wound. Once he was satisfied there was no further pus inside the wound, he sutured it and Nurse Fiona covered it with a clean gauze dressing. Patty remained perfectly still during this procedure too. Although her wounds were cleansed and dressed, the doctor was still concerned with her sunken eyes and emaciated body.

He asked Nurse Fiona to make sure she received some extra fluids and beef broth for nourishment. Nurse Fiona was the only nurse at Hillside that actually cared about her patients, and now that she was satisfied she had done all she could for Patty, she tended to her other patients. Lyle was working with her that day and he was an experienced orderly who had been employed by the previous owners of the asylum. He had been there for nearly fifteen years. He was far more intelligent and caring than most of the staff and one of the few that were able to read and write. Fiona always gave him extra responsibilities and he did what she asked without question. After he escorted all the patients into the dining area for tea, he returned to Patty's room with a bowl of beef broth and a cup of sweet tea. Although she still hadn't spoken since her treatment, he spoke to her as he gently fed her the broth. Patty managed to get through half the bowl and a few sips of tea. When he laid her back down in bed, he noticed a faint smile come over her face. Like Nurse Fiona, Lyle truly cared about the patients at Hillside, but he had a young family that depended on him and he knew that if he dared speak up on their behalf, his job would be in jeopardy.

Later that evening, Nurse Margaret returned for her shift and Fiona had purposely stayed behind to confront her about Patty's care. After a heated conversation which was mostly one-sided, Nurse Margaret promised she would not send Patty to the Preston Wing for any further treatments. Fiona left her with a warning that evening, "I better not find any faeces on Patty in the morning because if I do, you will be very sorry." Margaret didn't respond. Nurse Fiona left feeling much better than when she first arrived. Although exhausted from her long day at the asylum, she found it difficult to sleep that night. Nurse Fiona couldn't help but think what would have happened to Patty if she had taken more time off than she had.

Back in Elmvale, Lila made several attempts to reach Loraine Powel that evening but it wasn't until the following day that she finally got a response. Lila briefly explained what had happened to Patty Miller and Loraine could tell by her voice that she was extremely worried and anxious. Promising she would leave straight away helped to ease Lila's mind. Since losing her mother, Lila had moments when she felt uneasy about some of the decisions she made and now she truly needed her friend and mentor for moral support.

Now that she knew she was coming into town, Lila booked a room at Elmvale's only hotel and then went to see the editor of the *Elmvale Examiner*. She needed to know everything she could about the tragedy that had occurred at the Miller farm. Billy Carter had been the chief editor of the *Examiner* for over twenty years. He was a very experienced reporter and pretty much ran the entire operation single-handedly. Big Bill was his nickname, mainly because he was six foot two and weighed about three hundred pounds. Most folks described him as the kindest, most generous person in the entire town. He was such a character and loved by everyone who knew him. At Christmas he would dress up like Father Christmas and entertain the sick children at Orillia's Memorial Hospital. His long white beard and big belly had the children convinced he was who he said he was.

Every January he would set up a donation box inside his office and ask that each person wishing to speak to him leave a small gift behind for the needy children. This donation box sat in his office all year until it was overflowing with gifts. This was known by all the townsfolk, but unfortunately Lila hadn't been informed and when she asked Billy's secretary if she could have a word with him, the secretary asked where her gift was. Lila didn't have any idea what she was talking about, but when Jillian explained, Lila happily went across the street to the mercantile and purchased a wooden puzzle.

With the puzzle in hand she returned and was welcomed into Billy's office. Billy stood to greet her, his height was at least nine inches taller than hers and she felt a little intimidated by his stature. It wouldn't take long before Lila felt at ease around

Billy as she would come to admire his inner strength and integrity.

Billy was curious as to why this young woman, a perfect stranger and one that hadn't even been living in town when Patty was found, was so interested in the Miller case. Once Lila explained how she had come to know Patty, he offered to help in any way he could. Billy explained that he hadn't known Patty personally, but his heart was broken when he found out what happened to her and her infant son. He also felt that Chris should have been severely punished for what he had done, or neglected to do. Billy thought he should have hanged for allowing his child to die in such a painful manner and he told Lila he would like to have just five minutes alone with him.

After the two talked for a little over an hour, he offered Lila a small office that was currently being used for storage and told her she would have access to all of the *Examiner*'s articles on Patty and Chris Miller. He could tell that Lila was a strong woman and one that might expose Chris Miller for the kind of man he really was. He also suggested she go to the local constabulary and speak to Constable Blake; he was in charge of the investigation and could fill her in on any details that weren't documented in the articles.

That name rang a bell for Lila and then she realized it was Constable Blake that had investigated William Blows' disappearance and subsequent death. Lila had never been told the entire story about William's disappearance but she was still extremely relieved to know that he was no longer in Elise or Mavis's life. Although Lila had only met Elise's husband briefly when she was much younger, she did overhear her mother once say that Mr. Blows had been a cruel and heartless man who had brought his mistress into his marital bed.

Now it was time to concentrate on another heartless individual and get to the bottom of why Chris Miller was never given a lengthy prison sentence for his crimes. After sorting through at least thirty articles, Lila arranged them in order of date and time. Each one told a haunting rendition of wilful neglect and although they gave her insight into Patty's life after her mother had been taken to the hospital, they didn't tell the whole story.

In order to find out more information, Lila headed to the constabulary to speak to Constable Blake. As she walked to the constabulary that afternoon, she noticed Constable Blake arguing with a young woman and as she got closer, she thought she recognized her. When she heard Constable Blake say, "You ruined my marriage and my life, what more do you want?" right away Lila knew it was Catherine, the same woman that William Blows had been having the affair with when he went missing. Up until that moment Lila had forgotten all about this time in her life, but after hearing part of their conversation, she recognized Catherine's voice. Catherine had an extremely high-pitched voice and one that Lila would never forget. It was shortly after Charity was born when Lila had accompanied her mother to Elise's home when she first met this young lady. Catherine had come to the door that afternoon and was demanding to know where William was. Amelia became angry by her aggressiveness and stepped in between her and Elise and insisted that she leave immediately.

Lila didn't feel the least bit sorry for Constable Blake, his lack of restraint had caused his marriage breakdown and to her, he alone was completely responsible for the outcome. To bed a woman that was not your wife was a sin in Lila's eyes.

Now, as Lila waited for them to finish their conversation, she felt a deep sadness come over her. Had she just stayed in Elmvale perhaps none of this would have happened. Her mother might still be alive and maybe both of them could have done something to change the outcome of Patty's life. Lila had felt lonely after moving to London and most days Isaac was gone, leaving her alone with her infant daughter and her thoughts. Between caring for her daughter and her involvement with the suffragette movement she filled some of her time, but this didn't relieve her loneliness. Occasionally she would be called on to deliver a baby, but in London there were several midwives competing with each other and she felt left out most of the time. London was much larger than Elmvale and most people kept to themselves. Lila longed for the familiarity of small-town life and remembered the horrified look on her mother's face when she said she was moving away. She had also lied to her, telling her how happy she was, when in fact she was homesick each and every day. Now a grown woman, she realized that she had become just like her mother and she could no longer walk away when someone needed her.

Amelia had had a strong desire to fix everything and every-one. She would not stand back and watch women suffering at the hands of their husbands. Lila was only now beginning to understand why her mother felt compelled to give up her own life to become Patty's caregiver. Something inside her had compelled her to try and help Patty any way she could, even forsaking her own child to do so.

As she stood in the background, waiting to speak to the constable, she couldn't help but hear Catherine, who had raised her voice to such a degree that several police officers came out to see if there was a problem. She was demanding that Constable Blake increase his child rearing payments even though he often gave her money voluntarily. In Catherine's eyes it was never enough. Finally, after what seemed like an eternity she left and Constable Blake was able to go back inside the precinct. He didn't notice that Lila was following close behind and after several tries, she finally got his attention.

Constable Blake was in no mood to speak to anyone else,

especially another woman. As he turned to see who was calling him he soon changed his mind. Lila was a beautiful woman with a stunning figure, radiant smile and seductive blue eyes. After leaving Elmvale, she had blossomed into a lovely young woman who caught the attention of many young men. Constable Blake was attracted to her immediately. He didn't remember Lila as a young girl and thought she was a stranger in town, and he asked her to come into his office where they could have some privacy. He offered her tea which she accepted since she was parched after not stopping for any nourishment all morning. Once he understood why she was there he told her, "We tried to provide the best case for the Crown verses Chris Miller but the judge was far too sympathetic and let him go without so much as a fine. The Crown couldn't prove beyond a reasonable doubt that Chris Miller purposely and wilfully caused the death of his infant son or the poor condition they found his wife Patty in. He was released and has not been seen since." Constable Blake added, "As much as l would have liked to see him hang for this, l had to let it go and move on."

Lila asked, "Do you have any idea where he went?"

"Yes, l believe, he's now living on Christian Island with his mistress, Casandra Adams. If you are looking for Patty Miller, l think she was transferred to the Hillside Asylum after she was stabilized in hospital."

Lila was relieved to know that she had survived and thanked the constable for his time. Still, she was concerned when she heard where they had sent her. Asylums during this time were considered to be a last resort for most people, but she hoped that Patty was getting the care she deserved. It was only then that she remembered that she was to pick up Loraine, and she realized she was already an hour late. Now that she had the information she had been looking for, she planned on making a visit to Christian Island the following day. A visit to Hillside

Asylum was also in order but this would come at a later date. As she rushed to the train station that morning, all she could think about was what she and Loraine could do to make sure Patty and her son received the justice they deserved. Nothing would ever bring Ian back, but that didn't mean that his murderer should be allowed to go unpunished. Patty deserved closure and Lila planned on making sure that she got it.

5

Loraine was not in a very good mood when Lila showed up. It seemed the coal boy had fallen asleep and neglected his duties. The train stopped a half mile ahead of the station and the conductor felt it would take a while to get the fire going and suggested all passengers who were able to should walk the rest of the way. Loraine decided that the exercise would do her some good, but on her way into town she slipped down an embankment and lost one of her shoes in the river below. Lila didn't know whether to laugh or apologize so she didn't do either but when Loraine stepped in a puddle, she couldn't help herself and started to laugh.

Soon both women were in stitches, and as they walked toward the hotel arm in arm an older woman nearby scowled at them and called them harlots.

Loraine immediately stopped laughing, and before Lila could stop her she walked directly over to the old woman and said, "Excuse me, Miss, but it appears to me and my dear friend Lila that you have no sense of humour. Surely even a prune-faced old hag like you could manage a smile from time to time?"

Loraine then turned and walked back to Lila, who was now

laughing so hard she couldn't form a proper sentence. This was the first time Lila had smiled since hearing the news about her mother. It felt good just to let go of her thoughts, if only for a short time.

This behaviour wasn't unusual for Loraine and that's what attracted Lila to her in the first place. Loraine never held anything back and she reminded Lila of the way her mother used to be; a woman of strong convictions, and a mind of her own. As a suffragette that fought tirelessly for women's rights, she hated to see women being discriminated against, and she once got arrested simply for trying to make a point. Shopping downtown one afternoon with a friend, she walked into a private gentlemen's club that was strictly for men and proceeded to order a whiskey. When the bartender refused to serve her, Loraine refused to leave. A short time later the police were called and she was arrested for disturbing the peace. The next day, her husband bailed her out and he dropped her off back home. The minute he left for work, Loraine, along with Lila and two other women, went straight back and insisted they be served too. This time the owner gave in and served the women and after they finished their drinks, he insisted that they had to leave. Some of the men had already got up and left, but most stayed and didn't seem to be bothered by their presence. Loraine wanted the exclusive gentlemen's clubs abolished but this was not about to happen despite her protests. Later she was chastised by some of the other suffragette organizations for ever stepping foot in that place and she was also ridiculed for taking a drink. Loraine wasn't like the others; she was very independent and didn't mind that men drank alcohol, providing it was not in excess. In fact, Loraine often enjoyed a glass of wine with dinner and sometimes a sherry in the evening with her husband.

Once Loraine was settled into her hotel room, Lila explained everything she had learned up to now about Chris and Patty

Miller. Naturally, Loraine was horrified after hearing that Chris Miller just simply moved away, leaving his wife and infant son without food, water or even coal to heat her home.

She told Lila, "Chris Miller knew full well that he had no intentions of returning and that Patty could not survive on her own. Without the use of her legs she was confined to the house, unable to even walk the half mile to her friends' home or call someone for help." At the very least, Loraine felt that Chris needed to be brought up on charges and atone for his sins.

After listening to all the sordid details about what Patty and Ian Miller had endured during that time, Loraine decided she would join Lila the next morning to find out just what kind of a man Chris Miller really was. Lila was relieved to hear that Loraine was coming along, facing Chris on her own wasn't something she had looked forward to.

On the way home that evening, Lila couldn't get Patty off her mind. All she could hope for was that Patty wasn't aware of her son's suffering. Lila couldn't imagine how she would have felt knowing that her child was dying and there wasn't anything she could do about it.

Just as she arrived back at Elise's home, the sun had begun to set. As she unhitched her horse from the wagon, she glanced up at the window and could see Mavis gently rocking Isabel. Elise's children, Katie, Anne and Joseph, were sitting nearby and she could see that their mother was reading to them, something she had done each night since William died. Prior to his death, Elise was frail and unable to care for them properly. Now she was making up for that and vowed to give them a better start in life than she had had. The sight brought tears to Lila's eyes as she recalled how gentle her mother was with all the children in town. Now Lila was beginning to understand why Charity's death had broken her mother's heart and spirit.

When Lila went into the home, Katie, Anne and Joseph ran

to her. She was like a third mother and they felt as close to Lila as they had to Amelia. They had just been toddlers when she left for London, but Lila had visited frequently when she came into town to see her mother. It wasn't until Amelia stopped responding to her letters that these visits became less frequent. Still, the children recognised her right away and it was as though she had never left. Isabel was fast asleep and seemed content in Mavis's arms. After the children were in bed, Lila sat in the parlour chatting to Mavis and Elise. Soon Lila turned her attention to a picture of Elise, Mavis and her mother on the mantel. It was a lovely picture and it triggered some happy memories of a time not so long ago. Lila stared at it, wishing with all her heart that her mother was still in her life. The news about Patty and Ian had left her feeling sad and vulnerable and soon she couldn't hold back her tears. Elise went to her and held her tightly, it hadn't been long since she buried her mother and she could tell that Lila was missing her terribly.

After a restless night, Lila slipped out of the house unnoticed. The sun was just breaking through the clouds and she could hear the morning doves cooing in the distance. This sound was like music to her ears, something about these gentle birds felt calming and familiar. Lila took her time as she travelled to the Elmvale Arms Hotel to pick up Loraine. She watched as Jeremy Lions herded his sheep into the fields. She knew he didn't like her mother very much because she chastised him for not helping his wife take care of their seven children. Lila could see his wife, Emma, through the kitchen window and thought how nothing much had really changed in her hometown. The lilacs, her mother's favourite flower, were all in bloom and the scent reminded her of the time she stole a bunch off their neighbours' trees. Amelia didn't approve of stealing even if it was just a bunch of flowers, and Lila was forced to bring them back.

Lila laughed out loud as she recalled how Mrs. Crane insisted she keep the flowers and then gave her another bunch of lilacs to take home to her mother. Lila had been in such deep thought that morning that she nearly went right past Loraine, who was already waiting outside the hotel.

Their plan that day was to head to Christian Island, catching the first ferry at 0700 hours. Constable Blake didn't know the exact location of Chris Miller, but told her to speak to the manager of the mercantile, Richard Neely, as he knew everyone there and could direct her to Chris Miller and Casandra Adams. The short trip to Christian Island would take less than twenty minutes. When they arrived at the dock that morning, they were warned that the last ferry leaving the island was at 1300 hours. If they missed it, they would have to wait until the following morning. Neither of them expected to stay longer than an hour or so.

Lila had already decided to go to Hillside Asylum later that same day to see how Patty was doing. Although Lila had grown up less than twenty miles from Christian Island, she knew very little about the inhabitants. The island was a native reserve, surrounded by the clear blue waters of Georgian Bay. Known as a peaceful place where many families had lived for generations, it was currently going through a rough patch. Unfortunately, there had been a recent influx of migrant workers camping along the shoreline that belonged to the natives. This had caused some unrest, which in turn led to fighting and disharmony among the elders. Lila was warned by Constable Blake to stay away from certain areas there. Of course, Lila paid little attention to this warning; she didn't care where she had to go, once she got there, as long as she could expose Chris Miller in the process, that was all that mattered. Often fearless, Lila never thought of the consequences of her decisions until it was too late.

Georgian Bay was calm and still that morning as the ferry boat gently glided over the clear blue water. Lila was taken in by the beauty of the landscape that grew closer with each passing minute. Amelia had mentioned this beautiful island to her many times, but sadly, she had never had a chance to visit it.

The trip took less time than expected and the minute Lila and Loraine got off the boat, they noticed the mercantile that the constable had mentioned was just a few feet away from the dock. Richard Neely was a treasure trove of information and told the women exactly where Casandra lived, even drawing a little map, making it easier to navigate. Christian Island was not like most places, it did not have clearly marked trails, and after Richard rented two of the finest horses to Lila and Loraine, they began their long hike towards Casandra's property. The horses adapted easily to the uneven terrain and they were quite used to being ridden all throughout the island. The forest was filled with pine needles that morning; it had rained the night before and the smell reminded Lila of laying her head on freshly washed sheets that had been drying outside all day.

Once they finally spotted Casandra's home, they dismounted their horses and tied them to an old fence post nearby. It was easier to get there on foot than risk having one of the horses injured by the muddy, uneven path that led to her place.

Before they reached the front door, they were greeted by a young girl who introduced herself as Mary, the younger sister of Casandra. She told Lila that both Chris and her sister were down at the creek fishing and pointed towards a small opening in the bush. The area was too steep to ride through, so they carefully hiked down the quarter mile to the creek. This was a favourite spot for the locals, well hidden from the tourists and a great place to catch some trout.

It was Loraine who spotted them first and as she turned to see Lila close behind, she pointed in their direction and said, "It makes my blood boil watching that man enjoying life while his wife is living in a damned asylum!" The women could hear the couple laughing as they splashed water at each other, unaware that Lila and Loraine were now watching their every move. When Chris first noticed them, he just stared in their direction. It was obvious by the way they were dressed they weren't there to fish or explore the river and streams that washed into the bay.

Lila was the first to speak and, looking directly at Chris, she asked in a loud, demanding voice, "Do you know who l am?"

Chris replied, "No, but l am sure you will tell me."

Lila continued, "For your information, sir, I am Amelia Fern's daughter and l need to speak to you privately about your wife, Patty, and the death of your son, Ian."

The women watched as the colour drained from his face and it was clear Chris had thought that he had put that subject to rest.

Lila could tell that Casandra felt ashamed as she walked away and sat on a large rock overlooking the creek. Chris responded, "I have nothing to say; the case is closed so please, if you don't mind, just leave us be."

Lila raised her voice so Casandra would hear what she had to say. "So, Mr. Miller, you seem to have gotten on with your life while your wife Patty is left in an asylum, possibly for the rest of her days, and your child is lying dead in an unmarked grave! You, sir, couldn't even put out a few dollars to give your child a proper resting place!" She then looked at Casandra and said, "Are you sure this is the kind of man you want to spend the rest of your life with?"

Chris stood there wondering why this woman was harassing him, but he didn't say a word. Loraine then began, "You see, Mr. Miller, we are not going to stop until we have justice for your infant son and his poor mother! How do you think Patty felt knowing she could not save her child? How do you think she felt as she heard him whimpering in her arms?"

But Chris's only reply was, "Speak to my lawyer." Then he turned to Casandra and motioned her to follow him.

Lila and Loraine tried to follow them but they were too quick and soon disappeared into the forest. Both women rode back into town, seething inside. Lila wondered out loud how Chris could sleep at night. Once they got back to the mercantile, Lila went inside to speak to Richard. It was now almost lunchtime and many of the locals were inside gathering their supplies and chatting about the warm, humid weather.

Lila surprised everyone, including Loraine, when she suddenly climbed up on the counter and loudly announced, "People of Christian Island, 1 want to let you know you have a murderer among you. His name is Chris Miller and he is directly responsible for the death of his infant son and the deplorable condition his wife was found in."

Richard didn't know what to do, he seemed to be in shock as Lila certainly didn't fit the description he had in his mind of someone that would put herself on display as she had done. He insisted she get off the counter immediately and as he put his hand out to help her down, she pushed him away and continued her rant.

"Do you kind folks know what he has done? He abandoned his crippled wife and child, leaving them without nourishment or coal for the fire!" Just then Constable Patrick came through the door and ordered Lila to come off the counter or be arrested for disturbing the peace and trespassing.

Lila couldn't help herself and added, "He is guilty of murder and needs to hang for his crimes."

The officer then gave her one last warning and only after this, did she jump down and immediately apologise to Richard.

Lila felt somewhat vindicated afterwards but this was only the beginning, as she vowed to expose Chris for the man he really was.

Lila's statements had some effect on the locals as the minute she got off the counter, she was greeted by two elderly women who asked if what she said was true. Lila was eager to explain and said, "Yes, every word of it is the truth and we are going to make sure Chris Miller pays for what he has done."

The two women gasped and explained they were neighbours of Casandra Adams and her sister Mary. One of the women then told Lila that Casandra and Mary lived at the home by themselves after their parents had abandoned them a few years earlier. Casandra was nineteen now and she did her best to look after her younger sister, Mary.

Lila asked, "How often do you see Chris there?"

They both looked at her with an odd expression on their faces, then one said, "Oh dear, I guess you haven't heard, Chris and Casandra were married a few months ago."

Loraine abruptly pulled Lila aside and said, "He's not even divorced from Patty, surely that is an offence punishable by prison."

Realizing they had overstayed their welcome and were about to miss the boat, they raced to the dock to catch the last ferry back to the mainland. Lila was very satisfied with what they had learned and Loraine agreed it was a good start. If nothing else they could take this information to the police.

Once back on dry land, they decided to head straight to Hillside Asylum. The carriage ride would take less than an hour and they were both anxious to see Patty and make sure she was all right. Once they arrived, they both gazed up at the asylum and agreed it looked more like a prison than a hospital. This old rundown stone building was set back from the main road and surrounded by a large black rusty iron gate that was locked with three large chains. The bell barely worked, but Lila kept ringing it until one of the orderlies came out. Lila shouted through the door when she realized this man wasn't about to come to them. "I need to see a friend that has been admitted here, she is a very dear friend of my mother's and I need to know if she is okay."

The large, intimidating man shouted back, "Visiting day is the fifteenth of each month, come back then."

Lila looked at Loraine who seemed just as confused as she was. The fifteenth was another week away and Loraine interjected immediately, insisting it was of the utmost importance that she speak to their friend that day. The orderly walked away without acknowledging anything she said.

"Why can't we go in, what are you hiding?" Lila screamed, and was still screaming at the orderly when Loraine suggested they tie their carriage somewhere that was out of sight of the building and have a quick look around.

Loraine had no fear whatsoever, even though neither of them knew what they would find.

Once the horse and carriage were out of sight, the two women snuck around the back of the building where they saw several sections of the iron railings that had fallen down. They climbed through the opening and found themselves staring into a barred window.

When Loraine crouched down, she suddenly moaned, "Oh God, no."

She fell backwards onto the gravel. Too upset to speak, she just pointed at the window and turned away. Lila knelt down and was shocked by the sight of two naked corpses lying on a metal gurney.

Lila couldn't believe her eyes. Inside this dirty laboratory were two females lying face up with their eyes wide open. They both had their heads shaved and one had a metal rod stuck through her temple. Lila felt sick to her stomach and ran into the bush to vomit. The sight had frightened them so much that they retreated back to their wagon and immediately left the area.

On the way home, Loraine took Lila's hand and then said, "We must find out everything we can about Hillside Asylum, something very disturbing is going on in that place and we need to get to the bottom of it."

Lila agreed with Loraine and although she knew very little about this asylum, she had heard disturbing rumours about some of the others located north of Elmvale.

The rest of the journey was spent in silence as the women tried to make sense of what they had seen. When they got back to Elmvale, Loraine insisted Lila come to her room for a sherry before returning home. Lila accepted the offer; she was unnerved after what she had witnessed and wanted to calm herself down before she returned to Elise and Mavis. Lila told Loraine she had to know what was going on in that wretched place and, more importantly, she had to know what condition Patty was in. Since visiting days were only on the fifteenth of the month, they would have to wait another week before seeing her.

In the meantime, she told Loraine that she would check into the history of Hillside Asylum to see if there was any reason to be frightened for Patty's well-being. After another glass of sherry, Lila bid Loraine a goodnight and headed back. As she untied her horse and wagon a loud crack of thunder followed by lightning lit up the entire night sky. Lila quickly engaged her horse and they were on their way. The clouds opened up as she manoeuvred around several puddles not wanting to injure her horse or cause the carriage to overturn.

When she finally arrived back at Elise's home she was soaked through to the skin. All the lights were off in the house, except one in the kitchen. Lila had not noticed the time until she looked up at the clock hanging above the fireplace. It was almost midnight and she had missed another evening with her precious daughter. A note pinned to a dish towel that was sitting atop a large bowl read: *Isabel is an angel, she is sleeping in her cradle beside my bed, enjoy your dinner, love Mavis.*

Lila had no appetite, the sight at the asylum had left her feeling sick to her stomach. On her way to bed, she tiptoed into Mavis's room and gently kissed Isabel on the forehead before turning in for the night. Lila just couldn't relax and she couldn't get the vision of those two corpses out of her head. Her mind raced as she thought about how they got there and how thin they appeared to be, their cheeks sunken and their rib cages visible.

As she tried to sleep, she began to feel lonely without Isaac, but Lila was determined to stay in Elmvale and finish what she had set out to do. When she finally fell asleep, she dreamt of her mother who was standing in the shadow of a large willow tree. Lila ran to her, but she disappeared before her eyes.

Lila screamed, "Please, Mother, don't leave me again, I can't do this without you!" Her cries could be heard throughout the house and Elise came running into her room to try and calm her down.

Lila awoke in a cold sweat and found Elise sitting beside her, gently brushing her hair out of her eyes. "It's just a bad dream, sweetheart, now relax and get some rest, l will stay until you fall back to sleep."

Lila smiled and put her head on Elise's knee, soon her eyes closed and she drifted off into a deep, restful sleep. Thankfully, the dream didn't return that night, but it was so vivid that the next morning, Lila felt that the spirit of her mother had visited her and that she was still nearby, possibly watching over her.

Mavis and Elise had let Lila sleep in that morning, she hadn't touched her dinner the night before and they were beginning to worry about her state of mind. When Lila did emerge, she had large dark circles under her eyes – lack of sleep and worry was taking its toll. Mavis put some sweet bread in front of her and a large bowl of porridge. Although she picked at it, she hardly ate a morsel.

Lila told Elise and Mavis about her dream the night before as she sat holding Isabel tightly to her chest. Then she whispered, "I think my mother was trying to tell me something and I think she's here with us now."

Mavis and Elise looked at each other and smiled knowingly, then Mavis replied, "I know your mother is nearby, it was just a few days ago that I found a card she had given to me for Christmas a few years back, it was just sitting on my bed. Your mother had written me a message inside the card that read, 'Our friendship means the world to me. I hope you know that I will always be here for you.' She'd signed it, 'Your loving adopted sister, Amelia'."

Mavis said that the card had been tucked away inside her memory box which was on the top shelf of her cupboard and she had no idea how it had found its way to her bed that day.

Elise also had a story to tell. "The day after we were told your mother had died, I awoke with a dreadful headache. Amelia used to give me a few drops of opium when my migraines got very bad, but since she has been gone, I had to rely on aspirin tablets to ease the pain. Now, you are not going to believe this, but when I was getting dressed that morning, I glanced in the mirror and could swear I saw Amelia looking back at me. I rubbed my eyes and looked again but she was gone, and to my astonishment there was a tiny bottle of opium sitting right where I thought she had been."

Mavis interjected, "You see, Lila, your mother is with us all and now I am certain that she is very pleased to have you and her grandchild home again."

Lila was thrilled to hear the stories. She was very spiritual and did believe that in the afterlife spirits would seek out the people they were the closest to in life. It was also uplifting to hear that her mother continued to watch over both Elise and Mavis. They had been her closest and dearest friends in the final years of her life until Amelia became strangely obsessed with Patty Miller and slowly began to isolate herself from everyone, including her own daughter.

Lila was so thankful for both of them and she wanted to show them how grateful she really was. They had done so much for her and she felt like a part of their family. It happened to be a lovely warm day and Lila insisted they go to the movies. This was something they both loved to do but never had a chance since the children took up most of their time. Lila gave them both two dollars and told them to treat themselves to a nice lunch at the Elmvale Diner and not to rush back. The film *A Little Darling* was playing at the Fox Theatre and it was only there for two more days. At first Elise suggested they all go, but Lila reminded her how it would be if Isabel or one of the other children began to fuss. Elise agreed and without any further hesitation, the two women got ready to go. With that being said, Mavis and Elise left the house before Lila could change her mind. Having the children to herself that day took Lila's mind off the horrible sight she saw at Hillside Asylum. The children were the perfect distraction and being with them was the best therapy she could ask for.

Isabel was sitting up in her pram watching the butterflies in the tall grass and giggling at the faces Joseph was making. Isabel was beginning to resemble her mother, and Lila hoped one day to have a little sister or brother for her to grow up with. She wished that she'd had siblings, especially now that her mother and father were gone. There was not one family member alive that she could turn to, but still, she knew she was luckier than most.

A couple of the neighbours living nearby came out to greet Lila and the children. Some of the women knew her mother very well. She had delivered many of their babies and they were forever thankful for knowing her. Amelia was highly respected in the community, but she wasn't well received by some of the male population. Being a strong woman with an opinion about everything didn't help. She had a strong presence that most men thought of as unfeminine and crass. But Amelia hadn't cared, her only concern had been the babies she was birthing and their mothers. Amelia had once told Lila that men felt threatened by strong women.

She would say, "Do not conform to the belief that women were put on this earth to become slaves to their husbands, holding on to your independence is your God given right." Amelia never backed down if she felt that a woman was being ill-treated by her husband and she was never afraid to speak up when she needed to. Now Lila was about to follow the same path her mother had taken.

The day with the children was just what Lila needed and for the first time since arriving back in Elmvale, she slept soundly that night.

The following morning, she felt invigorated and decided to head to the library to research Hillside Asylum. Lila wanted to be well informed before returning to visit Patty. Although she had an overwhelming sense that something was terribly wrong at Hillside, she planned on going there with an open mind. Surely the corpses she saw in the cellar had died of natural causes and it was possible that they were just been stored there prior to their burial? Still, the rod protruding from one of their heads was something she couldn't fathom. If they had died naturally, why had that object been there? All these unanswered questions would be answered in time, but whether she was prepared for the answers was yet to be seen. For now, she was on a mission and with a fresh perspective and a good night's sleep, she hoped to begin to learn more about this strange place.

6

Patty had not said a word since her last electric shock treatments. Nurse Fiona was very concerned; it was as if Patty had given up entirely. She would only eat tiny amounts of food when she was coaxed but she usually fell asleep during this time. Weak and lethargic, Nurse Fiona checked on her regularly when she was on duty. In the meantime, there were other, more pressing issues to attend to. Lois had wandered away from her room and hadn't been seen for several hours. No one, not even her roommates, knew what had happened to her. According to one of the twin sisters, Lois had got up out of bed in the middle of the night and turned towards the stairs.

Rebecca had told Nurse Fiona, "It was very dark outside; I think it could have been three or four in the morning."

Although Rebecca wasn't exact about the time, she was correct when it came to the date as Lois was scheduled to have a bath that afternoon and wasn't available when the orderly came to get her. It was now the morning of June 15 and she still hadn't returned. Nurse Fiona wasn't too concerned for her safety; she worried more about the other patients she might encounter on her travels throughout the building.

Hillside Asylum was a massive building with two floors dedicated to patients and the ground floor where Mr. Potter had his office. The basement rooms were locked and off limits to all patients. This area, it was said, was used for storage but in reality this is where the Preston Wing had been purposely positioned, so the other patients and visitors couldn't hear the screams from the patients during the controversial electric shock treatments.

Distressingly, there was a huge number of people on the waiting list for Hillside Asylum and Mr. Potter was now insisting that Lois had abandoned her room. Without so much as a quick search through the entire building, he admitted a young girl named April Sampson to take Lois's place. Mr. Potter didn't care that Lois's room was paid in full for the entire month of June and, like so many times before, no one questioned his judgement, and no one would.

April had several deformities, but she was of sound mind. Her mother, a recent widow, just wasn't physically able to look after her any longer and had reluctantly decided to take the first available bed at Hillside. April required a lot of attention; she had no control of her bladder, little control of her bowels and one of her legs was shorter than the other one. This made it impossible for her to walk or even stand without leaning against a hard object. She had to be fed a special diet because she had brittle bones and at least twice a year she needed a plaster to support a fracture. April was very intelligent and although she was from a Dutch colony, she spoke fluent English with just a slight Dutch accent. She'd arrived in Canada when she was eleven years old, her parents hoping the doctors in Canada could help their daughter, but by this time they were given little hope that her physical conditions would improve in any way.

Now age nineteen, she was far too heavy for her mother to lift and without the means to hire a home nurse, she had no other choice than to commit April to Hillside for the remainder of her life. Home nursing would have been far less traumatic for April, but the cost was nearly double the amount per month of what Hillside was charging.

Out of all the patients that could have been placed in Patty's room, April, as it turned out, was the perfect choice. She was young, kind-hearted and patient and just happened to be the only one that would finally break through the protective wall that Patty had placed around herself. It began one afternoon, when Nurse Fiona noticed April sitting in her wheelchair next to Patty's bed.

April was reading one of her favourite books out loud. The story was about two young girls that were exploring a mysterious old castle together. It was filled with the misadventures of two teenagers that were so bored with their lives, that they often found themselves in precarious situations. At first, Patty just stared at the ceiling and April wasn't even sure she was listening. It wasn't until a rainy Sunday afternoon, less than a week after she arrived, when April began reading psalms from her Bible that she noticed a reaction from Patty.

April later told Nurse Fiona, "I put the book down to rest my eyes and Patty suddenly took my hand and said, 'please don't stop reading'."

Nurse Fiona was extremely pleased; she had been hoping that the latest shock treatments hadn't affected Patty's ability to speak. She told April, "Now you see, young lady, despite our circumstances, we all have a purpose in life, maybe yours is to bring joy to others."

April smiled shyly, she had never felt like she belonged and continually questioned her mother as to why she wasn't left to die when she was an infant.

Even though April really didn't belong at the asylum, there was even less room at the hospitals and no other places available that could take care of her special needs. April knew that it broke her mother's heart to relinquish her only child to Hillside, but she never blamed her for doing what she thought was best for her daughter. Sadly, it wasn't at all what she expected it would be and from day one, Rebecca and Adeline teased her relentlessly, sometimes bringing the poor child to tears.

Patty was frustrated with their behaviour and tried to come to her defence, but her vocabulary was limited, and she often jumbled her words, causing Rebecca to break into inappropriate laughter. As Patty became more insistent about knowing why she was in this place, Nurse Fiona enlisted Doctor Asher's help. His expertise in dealing with patients like Patty was invaluable and he began to spend a half hour a week with her explaining why she was there and gently telling her about her infant son.

She would react as expected to what he was saying, but the minute he left her room, she would ask Nurse Fiona the exact same questions, "Why am I here? Where am I?"

Doctor Asher believed she was purposely blocking out painful memories and this is when he ordered a controversial treatment. To remove the underlying cause of her hysteria, he decided to perform a lobotomy, severing the nerves to her frontal lobe thereby decreasing her anxiety. He and his colleagues had performed several and felt she would benefit from it greatly. Nurse Fiona wasn't convinced it was a good idea and since Doctor Asher was relatively new to Hillside, she didn't feel he was experienced enough. Reluctantly, she kept her opinions to herself. She knew if she wanted to maintain her position at Hillside, it was best to hold her tongue than to question her superiors.

7

L ila's attempt to visit Patty on the fifteenth of June failed
miserably as she had arrived late after experiencing an
issue with her wagon. Lila was furious, but nothing she said to
the attendants that day made one bit of difference, the opportunity to see Patty was no longer up for discussion. If not for her
determination and Loraine's persistence, she would have had to
wait until the following month. Still, it was almost three weeks
later before she received a letter stating that her application for a
"special visitors' pass" had been granted.

Now armed with the knowledge that she had uncovered
about Hillside's current owner, she was angry and frustrated
before she even arrived that day. Lila was now aware that Hillside had once been a place of refuge, a place where patients
actually recovered. When it first opened its doors in 1869, the
owners Joseph and Mable Hillside had only one vision and that
was to have a safe, clean home for people that society had given
up on. Joseph Hillside was a self-made millionaire, who had
worked at a farm as a young lad where he milked fifty cows
twice a day as well as maintained the property for the owner.
Joseph eventually persuaded his boss to try a new way of

milking the cows, something that would save farmers time and money. He had secretly invented a milk flow system, a simple pump action, tubed kit that attached to the udders of the animal and gently squeezed until milk flowed freely. Eventually his contraption was in great demand and after four years he sold the rights to a large manufacturing company.

It wasn't long after this that he met his wife Mable, a nurse in the Jackson Garden Sanatorium. Joseph had been visiting in the hopes that he could eventually admit his younger brother Jessie, who had been suffering from a deep depression. Joseph wanted Jessie to get all the help he needed and money was not a problem. Without many options available, he went to the only sanatorium that had space for another resident. Joseph was an intelligent man and after he toured the facility, he asked to speak to the staff alone. Mable was the only one who warned Joseph about the dangers inside the facility. He was so impressed with her kind demeanour and honesty that he began to pursue her, until she agreed to marry him.

Mable was also intelligent and when she spoke to Joseph about opening their own sanatorium, he jumped at the chance to help her. They both wanted a place that would exemplify patient care and understanding. Hillside Asylum officially opened its doors in July of 1869, their first admittance was Joseph's brother, Jessie Hillside. From 1869 to 1893 the facility ran very smoothly as patients that could do physical labour were given jobs and paid a small sum of money once a month. Some looked after the gardens, others cooked and cleaned and those unable to work were given small tasks.

The patients also enjoyed sitting outside on warm, sunny days and Joseph set up badminton nets, encouraging his residents to remain active. The middle-aged couple were loved by everyone; however, their good fortune wouldn't last. Joseph would eventually face a lawsuit, set in motion by another entrepreneur for stealing his idea. Joseph paid a very large sum of money to several lawyers, but still lost his case. The Hillsides had used most of their savings and eventually had no choice but to hand over the deeds to Hillside Asylum in 1893.

Andrew Potter, who knew nothing about running a sanatorium, purchased it and Jessie Hillside was removed immediately. Lila learned that since taking over the asylum, Mr. Potter had been in front of a judge sixteen times regarding complaints made about unethical care and abuse. Two other complaints were even more disturbing, after families of loved ones living in the facility reported that they were missing, neither one had ever been found. Due to the inability to prove that Mr. Potter was responsible for the missing patients or the unethical care, all he received was a small fine for the filthy conditions and a warning. The complainants hoped justice would be served and Mr. Potter would be held accountable but sadly, this was not the case.

On July 15, Lila was filled with anxiety as she now had to face her first visit to the asylum alone. When Lila arrived at Hillside, almost an hour early, she noticed two men standing in front of the gates. It seemed that she was not the only visitor that day and she wondered why they were stopping them from entering.

The orderly also insisted he check her bag before allowing her inside the gates. This seemed highly unusual but she complied. She would later learn that Andrew Potter was a paranoid man who thought that visiting days were unnecessary and that some visitors were there simply to spy on him.

Mr. Potter didn't have any compassion for his patients or the visitors, some of whom had to travel long distances. Just before she went inside the asylum, Lila noticed that the men that were behind her were being turned away. She couldn't help but hear one of them pleading with the orderly to let him inside, but Mr. Potter had just informed him that the patient they had come to see was deceased. These men had travelled all night on the train after receiving a call the day before that their nephew was ill, just to learn that he was already dead. This, Lila was told, was not unusual and although it was policy to inform the patients' families, Mr. Potter rarely let them know in advance. Unfortunately, they were also told they couldn't see him which also seemed highly unusual to Lila at the time.

Lila would learn a lot of disturbing things that afternoon. Despite being told not to talk to the visitors about Hillside, some of the orderlies opened up to her. Whether it was simply her kind disposition, or her ability to listen, Lila was able to convince some of the staff that she could be trusted. According to two of the orderlies, the residents were only bathed once a month and that was the day before visitors were allowed into Hillside. This orderly said it was to give the impression that the patients were well-cared-for. He also said that the dining area was scrubbed down and the corridor floors were washed, again, this was done only once a month to convince the visitors that the home was sanitary.

Lila certainly didn't think of this place as sanitary, the stains on the floors and foul smells that permeated throughout the asylum told a much different story.

Andrew Potter may have been a paranoid man, but he wasn't stupid. He put on a show for the visitors when they arrived each month and if his staff upset him in any way they were immediately dismissed. As Lila made her way to Patty's room that day, she heard faint screams coming from the cellar. These unnerving sounds made her wonder what was going on down there. Lila asked another orderly about the screams, but he told her that it must have been her imagination.

Lila replied, "I am not a stupid woman, I know what I heard and I want an explanation!"

The orderly then pointed to Nurse Margaret and told Lila she should talk to her. Lila asked, "What on earth is going on down there?" just as she heard another faint scream from below.

Nurse Margaret smiled sweetly, then said, "Oh, my dear, it's nothing to worry about. Some of our patients just hate having a bath and they tend to make a fuss."

But Lila wasn't convinced; she had seen the corpses in the basement and she still didn't have an explanation as to why they were there. Lila and Loraine had planned to find a way to investigate that further. In the meantime, Patty's well-being was her priority.

Patty was sitting up in her wheelchair and she smiled when she saw Lila come into the room. Her thin, emaciated body frightened Lila, but she tried her best not to react.

Lila now looked very much like her mother, Amelia, and for a moment Patty thought she recognized her. She spoke softly to Patty as she held her hands. "Do you remember me, sweetheart, I did come to your home at one time?"

Patty didn't answer and just focused her attention on Lila's wedding ring. Lila then asked, "How are you feeling, Patty, are they treating you all right?" Again, no response. Patty just turned away and stared straight ahead.

About ten minutes later Nurse Margaret came into the room to take Rebecca and Adeline downstairs to meet with the doctor. As she passed by Patty, Lila noticed her reaction, Patty closed her eyes tightly and cowered back in her chair as if she was about to get hit. Lila knew instinctively that Nurse Margaret wasn't the person she was trying to portray. Just as she was about to leave, Lila pulled her aside and asked, "Why is Patty so thin? She looks so frail now and I can recall a time, not so long ago, when she was of normal weight."

Nurse Margaret tried to act as if she was concerned too and said, "Yes I know, the poor dear just doesn't seem to have an appetite. We have tried everything to get her to eat but she is just not interested. It's possible that the shock of losing her child has had this effect on her."

Lila knew that Nurse Margaret was lying, Patty didn't even seem to remember anything that had happened to her or her child and if she had no recollection of his death, her current condition had to be from something else. Lila turned her attention back to Patty and asked her one more time, "Do you know who l am, Patty?"

Patty didn't seem to comprehend the question so Lila said, "Do you remember my mother, Amelia?"

Patty's eyes lit up and finally she spoke, "Why am l here, Miss? Did Amelia bring me here?"

"No, darling, Amelia would never bring you to a place like this, she loved you."

Patty then pleaded with Lila, "Please take me home. l don't belong here and I don't know where l am."

Lila's heart sank, Patty was far worse off than she suspected. Her body looked bruised and battered and she noticed her hair had been shaved off of both sides of her temples, a sure sign that electric shock treatment had been done. Although Lila wasn't personally familiar with this treatment, she had read about it in one of her mother's medical journals. Lila then asked one final question, "Do you remember what happened to your child, can you recall anything about him?"

Patty turned away from Lila as her eyes filled with tears. Lila could tell that deep down Patty had some recollection of what happened to Ian. Now Lila was filled with remorse. It broke her heart to see her like this and she knew that her mother would be devastated knowing what had become of her.

April, who had been sleeping when Lila arrived, sat up and

said, "You know, Miss, they are planning to do a lobotomy on Patty next month. I heard Nurse Fiona and Doctor Asher discussing it."

Lila turned towards April and asked, "Are you certain that's what the doctor is planning?"

April replied, "Oh yes, ma'am, I am very sure."

Lila thanked her for letting her know, she wasn't sure what to do to stop it, but she knew she had to find a way. Lila had a vague understanding of this invasive procedure and she felt that it was barbaric and totally unnecessary when it came to treating Patty Miller. A few seconds later a loudspeaker with a strong male voice interrupted their visit when he announced, "Visiting hours for our guests with special day passes is now over, kindly leave the building through the front doors."

Lila had only been there for an hour and she wondered why they wouldn't let her stay awhile longer. When the announcement came on again a few minutes later, she leaned over and hugged Patty tightly, then said, "It's time for me to go." As she stood up, Patty took her hand and held it against her chest, the look on her face was that of fright and confusion. Lila leaned down again and whispered in her ear, "Don't worry, darling, I will be back before you know it."

Patty slowly let go of her hand and watched as Lila disappeared into the hallway.

Lila left Hillside feeling that if Patty remained there, she would not live to see another birthday. She was appalled by what she had witnessed, and it was an understatement to say that Patty was in a grave condition. Lila also knew that the staff were lying about the screaming she heard coming from the basement. It was time to investigate further, and she felt she had to do something sooner rather than later. Lila had a plan and wanted to discuss it with the only person she knew that would understand.

Before heading to see Loraine, she went to the mercantile and purchased a child's gift. She needed to speak to Billy to see if he had heard any rumours about Hillside Asylum.

Billy Carter greeted Lila with a big smile. Unfortunately, when he learned why she was there his expression changed dramatically. Billy hadn't mentioned Hillside to Lila earlier because he wasn't sure if Patty had ended up there. At the time she was found, no one really thought she would survive and there were two other asylums being considered. According to Billy, Hillside was the worst.

He confessed, "I'm afraid that I have known about Hillside's terrible reputation for a very long time. Rumours of a mass grave had surfaced a few years back, but nothing was ever done about it. I suspected the doctors had been experimenting on some of the forgotten souls and I also heard that sexual misconduct had occurred between the male orderlies and some of the patients. In fact, one family eventually took their daughter out of Hillside because they noticed her belly growing at an alarming rate. When they took her to the infirmary, they found out she was with child. Mr. Potter denied all allegations of misconduct and blamed the patient's own brother for her condition. The family left the area soon after."

It was worse than Lila originally thought and she wondered why no one had been able to have the place closed down.

Lila immediately asked Billy if he would be willing to write her story. Without a thought for her own safety, Lila was planning on entering Hillside as a patient. If the rumours were true, she would expose the institution and its owner Mr. Potter for all to see.

Billy sat back in his chair, a huge grin returned to his face and he said, "If you are willing to take that risk then I promise you, l will not only write the story, l will do everything l can to make sure Mr. Potter pays dearly for what he has done."

But although this felt like the right thing to do at the time, Billy reminded Lila that it could be dangerous and told her to plan an escape route before being admitted into the asylum. He said, "Planning is the key to success. If you are as determined as l think you are, l know you will find the answers."

Lila thanked him for his time and told him she would be back when she was ready. Although Lila was very apprehensive about doing this, she felt that she didn't have any other options. Others had tried to expose Hillside for what it was and failed and she wasn't prepared to let this happen again.

Now a visit with her closest friend was in order, surely Loraine would support her in any way she needed. However, once Loraine heard what Lila was planning, she tried to talk her out of it. It was very dangerous and Loraine was worried that Lila could get hurt, or worse she could end up lying naked on gurney in the basement. Lila was very persuasive and after hearing about the dreadful condition she found Patty in, Loraine agreed to do whatever she could to help. The next thing to do, would be to convince Elise and Mavis that it was a good idea. Lila knew this wouldn't be easy.

There was another problem that neither of them thought much about. Hillside had a lengthy waiting list and Lila knew that if she had to wait another year or two that Patty would be dead. Moving Patty would have been the best option, if only her husband would agree to it. Shortly before Patty was transferred to Hillside, the Miller's home was sold and some of the money was put in a trust for Patty's care. Despite her husband's blatant disregard for his wife and his infant son, Chris Miller was given the authority to make decisions on Patty's behalf. Without his consent or an order from a qualified physician stating that there was some medical reason to transfer her, Patty could not be moved. Now Lila was determined to find a way to get her out of there, knowingly putting herself in harm's way in the process.

Thankfully, Loraine had connections and the first thing she planned to do was to contact her husband, Ernest. He was considered among the wealthiest men in London's high society and unlike most men of the time, he was a supporter of the women's suffragette movement. Since Ernest was friends with people from every walk of life, Loraine decided she would call him to see if he could find a doctor willing to make a false diagnosis. This was extremely important because without an actual reason for entering this asylum, Lila would be turned away. If Ernest was successful, she could get into Hillside without anyone becoming suspicious.

And if Lila could be portrayed as a woman of means, then Andrew Potter would be easy to manipulate. His focus was on making money and a little bribe could go a long way. Lila and Loraine were sure that this would help to get her to the front of the long waiting list. They now sat down with a glass of sherry and began to devise the perfect plan.

8

Back on Christian Island, Chris Miller was now being harassed by his neighbours and, feeling as though he was the victim, he put in a formal complaint to the constabulary, but they paid little attention to it.

Loraine was determined to keep up the harassment and contacted Constable Blake to tell him about the marriage of Chris Miller and Casandra Adams. Bigamy was a criminal offence, punishable by up to ten years in prison. Constable Blake promised that he would see Chris behind bars before the end of the Lord's year 1907. A few days later, Chris got word that the Elmvale Constabulary was about to arrest him and he fled the area, leaving behind Casandra who was now with child. Loraine and Lila knew he wouldn't stay away for long; he had little money and now everyone knew the story about him and Patty they all despised him.

Lila was still feeling distraught after her visit with Patty but the news of Chris Miller's impending arrest brought her some comfort. Although she felt that whatever prison time he received would never be long enough, at least his freedom would come to an end. Since seeing Patty, Lila was now even more convinced that he should hang for his crimes.

Over the next week, Lila talked to Elise and Mavis about her plan to enter Hillside. It took some time, but she soon convinced them that she would be perfectly safe at the asylum and she promised she would only stay as long as she had to. They in turn promised they would care for Isabel until Isaac arrived in mid-August. At this time Lila hoped to be home, but she didn't want to put a time frame on it just in case it took a bit longer than expected. If Lila felt that her life was in jeopardy in any way she had a plan to escape in place. If at any time life in Hillside became too difficult, Lila would get a message to Loraine, then have her get in touch with the doctor in London who would immediately issue a transfer to another facility.

Lila believed that this was foolproof and now that everything was set in motion, thanks to Loraine's husband, she would officially become a resident of Hillside on July 30, 1907. This would give her sixteen days to find out everything she could about Hillside and their staff. Loraine agreed to fund the entire scheme and, to Lila's surprise, she also offered to have Doctor Lloyd, a personal friend, see that Patty was transferred into a proper facility so she could receive the care she desperately needed. Having a doctor order this transfer would mean that they would not need Chris Miller's permission to do this. This transfer would take place the following month and they hoped to have Patty settled in Stafford Creek Sanitorium by August 23. This was a privately funded sanatorium located on the outskirts of town. It was well known for catering to the rich and was considered a place where one could come and get the best possible care. Stafford Creek employed two well-known published psychiatrists and an array of caring and devoted nurses.

Lila was thrilled when she heard where Patty was going and very thankful to Ernest and Loraine because without their generosity, Lila wasn't sure what would become of Patty Miller. Disturbingly, the divide between the haves and have-nots was huge. For those that couldn't afford a place like Stafford Creek, they often ended up in the most horrid conditions imaginable.

But now, thanks to Loraine and Ernest, Patty would soon receive the care she deserved. Lila admired both of them and described their marriage as one from a fairy tale. It was full of romance and passion with an enormous amount of trust and respect for one another. Ernest was a lovely man and devoted husband, and he also happened to be an extremely handsome fellow. Loraine loved Ernest dearly, he was the perfect husband for a suffragette wife; always supportive of whatever cause she was fighting at the time.

Lila and Loraine went over the plan several times after Doctor Albert Lloyd had sent a request for admission to the Hillside Asylum for his patient Lila Fern. Ernest also personally contacted Andrew Potter and after they discussed the possibility of a generous donation made on his sister-in-law's behalf, Mr. Potter agreed to find a room for her. Lila would be admitted by her wealthy sister, Mrs. Loraine Powel; her diagnosis was severe depression and hysteria.

As Lila prepared herself, she changed her entire look, including cutting off most of her hair and eliminating make-up entirely. She also purchased some oversized frocks from the charity shop. This was to make her look thinner and slightly dishevelled. Her entire look had changed and Lila was pleased with the results. Like her mother, Amelia, Lila was extremely stubborn and determined. She never turned away from an injustice, just because it might be difficult to resolve. The moment Elise, Mavis and Loraine saw her, they couldn't believe their eyes. She looked like a vagrant that hadn't eaten in days and now everyone was certain that no one would recognize her from her previous visit at the asylum. This gave Elise and Mavis some solace. If Lila was recognized then her life could be in danger.

~

The morning of July 30 was bittersweet for Lila. This would be the first time since Isabel was born that she would be without her mother for more than a day or two. Mavis and Elise promised to take good care of her, and they also made Lila promise that if she felt threatened in any way that she must send a message to Loraine immediately. After a long goodbye, the ladies left for Hillside. Although Lila was nervous, she never once complained.

Sadly, Lila had been jealous of the close relationship her mother had with Patty and when her mother stopped responding to her letters, she mistakenly assumed that she had turned her back on her. If only Lila had realized at the time that her mother's mental state was in question, then maybe things would have been different. Ian would still be alive and Patty certainly wouldn't be in an asylum. As they arrived at the gates, Lila took a long, deep breath before Loraine rang the bell. Once inside the asylum they were greeted by a very pleasant young girl who asked them to wait in the sitting room for a few minutes. Both Lila and Loraine felt a little nauseated as they immediately noticed an overwhelming smell of urine and faeces permeating throughout the building. Mr. Potter really didn't like getting involved with the patients, but he insisted on meeting all new ones before they were admitted to Hillside, making sure the patients knew he was in charge.

As they sat waiting to be called into his office, Loraine held Lila's hand and said, "You know, my dear, you don't have to do this."

Lila smiled and replied, "But I do, Loraine, I must know what is going on here and why Patty is so poorly. Besides, you know my mother would have done the exact same thing."

A few minutes later, Mr. Potter came out to greet them. He was nothing like either of them expected. Andrew Potter was a tall, handsome fellow who spoke with a slight Scottish accent. He appeared to be in his early thirties and Loraine also noticed that he was wearing a very expensive, fine tailored suit and a gold pocket watch that he checked several times during their interview.

Loraine was also surprised at how educated he seemed as he explained in some detail as to what his patients could expect during their stay at Hillside. During this time, he did not acknowledge or speak to Lila as she sat with her head down. Once he read the admittance letter from Doctor Lloyd, he called for an attendant. Luckily, Lila would be just a few doors down from Patty. She would share her room with Esther and Gladys, two middle-aged women, both admitted to Hillside for having impure thoughts.

A few minutes later, Lila was whisked away by an orderly, she did not turn back to look at Loraine.

Loraine left feeling very uneasy about leaving Lila there and on her way back to the hotel, she stopped in to see Billy at the *Examiner* to let him know how the morning had gone. With a pencil case in hand for his gift box, she entered his office.

Billy had promised Lila that he would not write a word about Hillside until she was safely out of the asylum and he'd got the whole story. However, he did require updates each week until her release. When Loraine told Billy about Andrew Potter's demeanour that morning, Billy wasn't surprised.

"I heard rumours about Mr. Potter's personality; he's also known for being a womanizer." He added, "Mr. Potter's worth a lot of money, and I found out some interesting facts about his assets. It seems he has interests in several other properties, which are scattered from Elmvale to York."

Loraine enjoyed talking to Billy, something about his friendly and animated demeanour made her feel comfortable around him. Before leaving his office that day, Billy had one request, he wanted to join Loraine when she visited Lila on the August 15, he assured her that he would disguise himself.

Loraine agreed that he should come along, she hated the thought of going alone, but she wondered how Billy could change his looks since he was hard to mistake. His sheer size alone was very unusual and few men in the area were as imposing as he was.

Later in the afternoon, Loraine rushed over to let Mavis and Elise know that Lila had been admitted and that everything had gone according to plan. She reassured them by saying, "Now don't you worry, l will make sure no harm comes to Lila. In fact, l have already spoken to an orderly and offered him five dollars to come by my hotel and let me know how Lila is doing."

When Elise asked, "How can you be sure he's trustworthy?" Loraine answered, "Five dollars is a great deal of money, especially for a lad who is making ten dollars a month."

9

B ack at Hillside, Lila was taken directly to the delousing room. She was stripped of her clothes and made to endure a cold bath, all the while being watched by an unknown male orderly. Nurse Margaret seemed to have no idea who she was and took an instant disliking to her. During her bath, she scrubbed her skin over and over again with lye soap causing it to erupt in a red, blotchy rash.

When Lila had finally had enough, she said, "You're hurting me, surely if I had lice, they would all be dead by now."

Nurse Margaret laughed, then replied, "Just shut up, or I'll give you something to complain about."

She then forcefully pushed her back in the tub until her hair fell into the water, a foul-smelling shampoo was applied to her scalp and as Margaret stood back, she said, "Now work that through your hair or l will cut it all off!"

Lila did what she was told and watched as the orderly went through her belongings, tossing most of it on the dirty floor. To her surprise, she saw Margaret tuck one of her nightdresses into her medical cart. This particular nightdress had been given to her by her mother and it was the one she always wore when she was feeling anxious. Now she wondered why Nurse Margaret was putting it into her cart, but Lila didn't dare ask. A few minutes later the nurse returned to the bath and told Lila to rinse her head then get out of the tub.

Lila was shivering uncontrollably, but she did her best to get all the fowl smelling shampoo off her scalp. Now satisfied it was gone, she looked around for a towel before standing up. Lila was feeling vulnerable as the orderly had turned his attention back to her. She had tucked her legs up into her chest to conserve heat hoping that the nurse would bring her a towel.

A few seconds later, Nurse Margaret stood over her with her arms folded and said, "What the hell are you waiting for?"

Lila looked up and replied, "Can't you see I need a towel?"

The nurse exploded into inappropriate laugher, but soon her whole demeanour changed completely as she leaned down and grabbed her arm, forcefully yanking it until Lila stood up. Lila tried desperately to cover herself as she stood there for what seemed like an eternity, waiting for something to dry herself with. Margaret was busy having a private conversation with the orderly before finally coming back with a dirty, damp towel. She threw it in her direction and then laughed when she saw that part of the towel had fallen back into the water.

Lila did her best to dry herself and not react to what Nurse Margaret had done. All she wanted was to put some clothes back on and get as far away from this nurse as she could. The towel was useless so instead of even trying to dry herself, she reached for her clothes that were sitting on the dirty, wet floor beside the tub. Before Lila could get her frock over her head, Nurse Margaret came over and slapped her hand, then screamed, "Don't touch those, they need to go into a special wash." She then handed Lila a plain blue frock that was labelled "Hillside" and told her to wear one of these at all times. She laughed as

Lila tried to put this on without exposing herself. There was absolutely no privacy and both Nurse Margaret and the unknown orderly seemed to enjoy watching her struggle. Still, Lila held her tongue and decided it was best not to complain.

When her ordeal was finally over, Lila was taken to her room. Esther and Gladys greeted Lila with a smile as she arrived, but the minute they saw Nurse Margaret they both turned away. After pointing to her bed, the nurse said abruptly, "You are allowed one blanket, if you soil it, lose it or ruin it in any way your family will be expected to pay for a new one, do you understand?"

Lila had had enough of Nurse Margaret and she really wanted to smack her for being so miserable that morning, but again she held her anger inside and did nothing. Nurse Margaret seemed to enjoy the power she had over the patients at Hillside and this would become more apparent with each passing day.

Once she left, Lila was finally able to speak to Esther and Gladys about their stay at Hillside. Both women vehemently denied having impure thoughts. According to Esther, her husband, Robert, was tiring of her and simply wanted her out of his life so he concocted a story about his wife having impure thoughts and justified putting her into the asylum. Gladys's husband, Cedric, wanted a divorce and she refused, so like Esther's husband he concocted the same story, placing her in Hillside after convincing a psychiatrist that she was acting more like a prostitute than the woman he married. Sadly, she also had to give up her rights to her children, which made Lila very angry. She wondered what her mother would have done to help this poor woman, but like Elise always said, "Remember, child, you can't save the world." Lila knew that there was little she could do for her now, as she concentrated all her efforts on learning everything she could about what was really going on at Hillside Asylum.

Neither one of these women seemed to be unstable, but Gladys did have tremors and told Lila she had been given two electric shock treatments since she arrived at Hillside for apparently being defiant. Both of these treatments had been set in motion by Nurse Margaret.

Once Lila was settled, she snuck down the hallway to Patty's room. Thankfully, April didn't recognize her and neither did Patty who was lying in bed staring at the ceiling. It wasn't long before Lila noticed a burn on her arm and asked, "How did this happen, Patty?" Patty didn't answer and continued to look straight ahead. Lila then turned to April and asked the same question.

After a long pause, April replied, "I wish I knew, Miss, but one day when I was in the dining area I came back and found Patty screaming in pain, her arm was clearly burnt and she wouldn't tell me how it happened. Patty was very upset but when I called Nurse Margaret, she didn't seem concerned."

Lila really liked April; she was intelligent and very caring and she felt that she could trust her. Patty was still staring at the ceiling when Lila went over to April's bed and whispered, "Can you keep a secret?"

April smiled and replied, "Yes, of course you can trust me, Miss."

Feeling confident she would keep her secret, Lila again whispered in her ear, "My name is Lila Fern, the same woman you saw here awhile back. I'm here to help Patty, now promise me you won't tell a soul."

April promised her, then said, "Please, Lila, can you help me too? I think I will die in here if you don't help me find a way to get out."

Lila smiled, gave her a hug and said, "Yes of course I will."

April had been very upset because her mother hadn't written to her like she promised she would. Since coming to Hillside, April had been beaten by Rebecca, her Bible had been stolen and sometimes she was forced to lay in bed all day because no one had come by to help her into her wheelchair. Lila did notice that like Patty, April didn't look very well and the frock she had on was stained and smelled of urine. It looked like it had never been changed since the last time she had seen her.

After assuring April that she would find a way to get her out of Hillside, she turned her attention back to Patty. Lila sat on her bed beside her and asked, "What are you thinking about, sweetheart?" Patty slowly turned towards her, her eyes were dark and sunken back into their sockets and the sight of her frightened Lila, but she tried very hard not to react.

In a barely audible whisper, Patty replied, "I don't know why I'm here, or where I am. Can you tell me, Miss?"

Lila held her hand and replied, "You are at Hillside Asylum, and one day very soon you will be gone from this wretched place." Just then Lila saw a look of fear come over April's face and turned to see Nurse Margaret standing in the doorway.

Lila stood and tried to leave, but Nurse Margaret stood in her way and said, "Now, Lila, tell me, what are you doing in here?"

Lila put her head down and said, "Oh sorry, nurse, I thought this was my room."

Margaret moved away, allowing her to leave, but warned her, "Stay out of here, if you know what's good for you!"

As she hid in the corridor, she overheard Nurse Margaret chastising April for staying in bed, then she heard the nurse scream, "Patty, look at me when I'm talking to you, have you learned nothing since arriving here?"

Lila didn't want to be seen and when she heard the nurse tell April she would be back soon, she quickly headed to her room. Inside the rather cramped bedroom, she found Esther and

Gladys were playing cards. The game had no rules and Lila couldn't follow along, but the ladies just laughed and continued to play. Boredom was a problem in the asylum as most days the only time the patients left their rooms was for meals. The sound of patients crying out echoed through the halls and Lila knew that she couldn't stay there any longer than she had to. It was now easy to see how this horrible place could change someone, or even cause someone to lose their mind.

An hour after returning to her room, Lila heard the sound of two extremely loud bells. The noise was so intense that it had caused her to jump up and run into the hallway. This is when she noticed a large number of patients walking in one direction. It was all very strange as none of them said a word as they passed by her.

At first, Lila had no idea what the bells meant. After watching this rather odd occurrence, she went back into her room to see Esther and Gladys coming towards her.

"It's time for tea," Gladys announced, before following the rest of the patients down the corridor. As she followed the ladies down the hall, she peaked inside Patty's room and saw that she was still laying on her bed staring at the ceiling. A few minutes later, they came to a large room only to see that the rest of the patients were now pushing and shoving their way into the door. Esther told Lila not to react if someone pushed her or went in front of her. She said, "Some of these people would cut your heart out for less than a piece of stale bread, so be careful not to upset them."

Lila then became distracted when she noticed Nurse Margaret wheel Patty into the dining room. Just behind her, an orderly wheeled April in and placed her in the line-up. Instead of staying to make sure these two helpless girls got their meal that day, they just left them there. Lila was appalled, neither April nor Patty were capable of holding a tray and wheeling themselves back to a table. Patty was barely capable of feeding herself. Now Lila understood why Patty was so thin, and why April had lost weight since her last visit. Lila decided that as soon as she got her meal she would go back to the line and help Patty and April with theirs.

Gladys found a quiet spot where they could eat in peace, and Esther promised to let Lila know if she saw Nurse Margaret come back. Lila was disgusted by the dining area, her feet stuck to the floor as she walked down the line and rat droppings were everywhere. It also looked as if the tables hadn't been cleaned in ages. It was so unsanitary that she was beginning to lose her appetite. After being pushed around and screamed at for being in the way, Lila came in front of the server where a plate of watery beans was pushed towards her. The next server gave her a piece of stale bread and lastly, she was given weak tea to wash it down with. Once she sat her tray at her table, she returned to take both April's and Patty's but was told by a server to let them be. Lila refused and insisted she carry the tray, telling the server, "Neither one of these girls can manage to carry their trays and wheel themselves to a table, even you can see that this is impossible, can't you?"

One of the other servers intervened. "Give her their trays, she'll learn soon enough!" Lila picked up Patty's tray as the girls serving food broke out in laughter behind her. Once she had April set up, she returned to Patty's table where she attempted to help her with her meal. Just as she held the first watery spoonful of beans up to her lips, Lila felt someone grab her by the arm. Believing it was a patient, she pulled her arm back only to find that her hair was now being pulled. Lila turned to swat the person away and found Nurse Margaret and an orderly standing behind her. A few seconds later she was dragged by her hair into the hallway. Both Patty and April cowered in fear, unsure what they were going to do to Lila. Because the patients were terrified of Nurse Margaret, no one ever stood up to her, so neither Gladys nor Esther came to Lila's defence.

A half hour later, three bells were heard, and all the patients hurried back to their rooms, some leaving their uneaten meals sitting on the filthy tables. When Gladys and Esther returned to their room, Lila wasn't there and neither of them knew where Nurse Margaret had taken her.

Lila had no idea what was going on and as she attempted to pull herself away from the orderly's grip, Nurse Margaret yanked her hair harder, pulling several strands out in the process. Now terrified of what she was about to endure, she began to pray.

Lila had only just arrived and Gladys and Esther prayed that she hadn't been taken to the Preston Wing. Unfortunately, this is exactly where Lila would end up. The procedure was completely uncalled for, yet somehow, Nurse Margaret had convinced the doctor it was necessary. To justify the shock treatment Lila would have that day, she would write in her nursing notes, "Lila Fern was extremely disruptive in the dining room today and when I asked her to behave herself, she spat at me and then tried to strike me with her tray. I suspect that she will be a troublemaker." Everything that the nurse had told the doctor was a pack of lies, but neither the doctor nor the orderly that had assisted her in bringing Lila downstairs, questioned her decision.

At 5am the next morning, Lila was returned to her room by two orderlies. Lila's face was red and swollen and her hair had been shaved off on both sides of her head. One of the orderlies carefully placed Lila on the bed, then quickly left the room. Esther was so concerned by the way she looked that she immediately went to her side. Lila was unconscious and she didn't respond to her voice.

She would end up sleeping for fifteen hours, before being awakened abruptly by a loud scream that was coming from the room next door. Lila tried to stand to see what was happening, but her legs felt like pudding and her balance was completely off. Gladys told her that one of the patients had stolen something and was being taken to the "quiet room" for punishment. Lila could hardly comprehend what she was saying and asked, "How long have l been asleep, is Patty okay?"

Gladys replied, "It's been about fifteen hours; you know we were really getting worried about you."

Lila had no recollection of what happened. The last thing she remembered was Nurse Margaret taking her into the basement. At this point she was feeling light-headed and weak. Lila hadn't eaten or had anything to drink since being admitted to Hillside. Her throat was terribly dry and her lips were red and cracked.

A little while later, a nurse she hadn't seen before came in; her name was Daisy Foxwell. Nurse Daisy seemed agitated when she saw Lila and asked with a commanding voice, "Why are you still in bed? It's nearly six o'clock in the evening and now you've missed your tea."

Lila could barely get any words out, her thoughts were jumbled but she managed to say, "l have a headache." Nurse Daisy picked up some soiled clothing off the floor, then left without saying another word. It wasn't until about two in morning before she awoke again, but this time it was to discover an orderly standing over her. At first, she was frightened and gasped when she saw him, but once she could focus on his face, she realized he was the same young man that Loraine had hired to report back about her condition. He whispered, "Lila, my name is Josiah and 1 am a friend of Loraine's, is there anything 1 should tell her?"

Lila was still confused but managed to say, "Yes, 1 think they gave me electric shock treatment."

"Yes, they did, Lila, 1 was the one who put you to bed afterwards."

"Please tell Loraine, it is much worse than I thought, and I might not be able to stay the duration."

Josiah promised he would and before he left, he said, "1 will drop in on Tuesday night. Now be careful, Lila, one never knows what might happen in here."

Lila turned back over and tried to get back to sleep. She drifted in and out of the same dream she had recently and once again saw her mother standing under a willow tree. Lila tried to run to her, but her legs wouldn't work and she called out, "I can't seem to move, Mother, please can you come to me?" Just as she got the words out, Amelia disappeared into the woods.

Lila began to sob and her cries woke Gladys who then attempted to comfort her. She opened her eyes and it took her a few minutes to realize where she was. Like before, the dream was very vivid and it seemed so real to her that she began to feel at ease, believing her mother's spirit was still with her.

10

Lila received a response from Josiah as promised. Loraine had written back, "My dearest friend, just tell this lad if you want me to get you out of there, please don't risk your well-being." Giving up just wasn't in Lila's nature and despite everything that had happened to her since her arrival, she was determined to see this through to the end.

Lila was feeling a little stronger now and her message back to Loraine was, "I never meant to worry you, I was just feeling vulnerable, but now I am much more focused and l still need to investigate further. I can say one thing for sure, there is definitely something very wrong in here and I suspect that Nurse Margaret has a lot to do with it."

Josiah tucked the note into his pocket and left without being noticed. He couldn't risk being found out and he knew that Nurse Margaret was in charge that evening. Lila also feared she would be watching her closely. For some unknown reason, she seemed to have more say at Hillside than the other nurses.

The following day, Lila had regained enough strength to take a little walk down the hall and attend breakfast. She had now been at Hillside for four days and because she had been incapacitated, she hadn't learned as much as she would have liked. Despite having gone through the unnecessary and barbaric electric shock treatment, Lila did not feel sorry for herself. She knew the risks when she entered Hillside and this only convinced her to delve deeper into finding out all the secrets the asylum was hiding.

Now feeling more like her old self on the way to the dining room she went to check on Patty, but she wasn't in her room. A quick search of the dining area didn't reveal Patty's whereabouts either. It wasn't until she saw April later that morning that Lila learned the truth.

"Doctor Asher was here earlier with Nurse Margaret and I saw them speaking to Patty, but I couldn't hear what they were saying."

Lila asked, "Do you think he is doing the procedure earlier than expected?"

April put her head down and replied, "Yes, Lila, I think he is."

Lila felt helpless, she knew there wasn't anything she could do for Patty now except wait and worry.

Once Lila returned to her room, she suddenly recalled someone mentioning the "quiet room" to her, but she couldn't remember who it was. Lila asked Esther and Gladys if they recalled this place and both women shuddered when she mentioned it.

Esther then asked, "Don't you recall being woken up by screaming the other night?"

Lila remembered hearing someone screaming but didn't pay much attention to it because it happened all the time there. She then asked, "What does that have to do with the quiet room?"

Esther looked at Gladys who shook her head as if to say "tell her", then replied, "Mona Sharp had stolen a towel from the bathing area, and when Nurse Margaret found it under her pillow she called the orderly to take her to the quiet room."

Lila said, "Why was she screaming, were they hurting her?"

Esther's tone softened, before she answered. "We have both experienced the quiet room. It is a place with no windows in the dank corners of the cellar." A tear came rolling down her cheek as she added, "There is a chain fastened to the cold stone wall that they attach to your arms, you cannot move or change position the entire time you're there and the pain in your shoulders becomes so unbearable that you pray for death."

Lila's expression changed from anger to sadness, then she asked softly, "And how long are you held there?"

Esther was now too upset to speak, and she began sobbing, so Gladys answered, "Until they think you have learned your lesson. One day, sometimes two, sometimes more."

Lila was shocked by this information and she planned on giving Josiah a message to bring to Loraine about what she had just learned. It seemed to her that the basement hid Hillside Asylum's dirty little secrets and with this in mind, she decided it was time she saw for herself what was going on down there.

Lila knew that this may be a foolish and dangerous move on her part, but that wasn't about to stop her. Considering how frail Patty was and now watching April's health decline, time wasn't on Lila's side. She truly believed that this was something she had to do. Something that just might save Patty's life and possibly more of the unfortunate souls that called Hillside their home.

Late that same evening, Lila pretended to be asleep when the night nurse came around to do her last rounds. She was one of few nurses that didn't hide in the lounge downstairs and sleep through her shift. A few patients still wandered the halls, but they were so medicated they didn't even notice Lila leaving her room. With only the dim light from her lamp, she slowly made her way down to the basement, making sure none of the staff saw her leaving. The minute she got down there, she could feel the dampness and smell the mould that lingered throughout the asylum. The long, dark corridor seemed to go on forever, door after door of rooms that were in complete darkness. As Lila passed by one of those rooms, she heard someone screaming. The sound was so unnerving that she initially contemplated running back to her room.

After a few minutes the screaming stopped and Lila decided that she couldn't just ignore what she had heard and now, despite her fear, she needed to find out what was going on inside the room. The heavy metal door was locked and as much as she tried, she couldn't gain access. As she stood there trying to figure out how to get in, she could still hear someone crying inside. Lila did the only thing she could and knelt down on the dirty cement floor as she peered through the keyhole. At first, she had no idea who was inside the room, but as her eyes adjusted to the dim light, she could clearly see a woman lying on a steel gurney. Like the two deceased women she and Loraine had seen through the back window, this woman was also completely naked. Lila tried to focus in on her face and saw the numerous scars left behind from picking the scabs from her face. Was this the woman that Esther had told her about? The one that shared a room with Patty before she suddenly disappeared? Lila only knew this poor soul by her first name, it was Lois. Her thin, emaciated body exposed her rib cage and it appeared as if her arms and legs were tied down, making it impossible for her to move. Lila wanted to free this woman, but just as she stood up to see if she could find something to open the door with, she heard the sound of someone's footsteps coming towards her. Lila had to put out her lantern, fearing she would be seen and possibly caught in a place that she knew was off limits.

As she hid in the dark corridor trying to be as quiet as she could, she thought she saw Nurse Margaret and Doctor Asher entering a room close by. Lila nervously waited for them to leave and as she stood in the darkness, she felt a rat run over her bare feet several times. Knowing Nurse Margaret was close by, Lila didn't move or cry out even though the thought of what just happened made her feel sick to her stomach. Lila's heart was racing and she broke into a cold sweat, as the fear of being discovered increased with each passing minute. After waiting for what felt like an eternity for them to leave, another rodent brushed by her leg. Lila couldn't stand it any longer and decided it was time to go. As she slowly felt her way along the dark corridor she tried to be as quiet as possible. Lila could hear Doctor Asher and Nurse Margaret in a room two doors down from where she had seen Lois. The door was slightly ajar and she could hear what sounded like two lovers engaging in sexual relations. Only now was she beginning to see why Nurse Margaret had so much leverage in Hillside.

A few minutes later, Lila finally found the door that led back upstairs. As she slipped out unnoticed, she could hear the doctor and Nurse Margaret coming towards her. Lila ran as fast as her legs would move and hid behind a chair in the lobby, her breathing was laboured and she felt dizzy and light-headed. The effects of the electric shock treatment were still present and she knew if she didn't get to her room very soon, she would pass out and be found behind that chair. As she waited and watched, she saw the two of them embrace, then begin kissing one another passionately.

Lila waited until they finally left the building together and after making sure they weren't coming back; she made her way to her room without being seen. Both Esther and Gladys were fast asleep as she slipped under her blanket and tried to get the image of Lois out of her mind. The sight had left her queasy and a wave of nausea came over her. Feeling like she was going to be sick, she got up and went to the window for some air. The window was open a few inches and although it was dark outside, she could make out the silhouettes of two men walking towards the forest. Lila couldn't be sure but for a moment she thought the taller of the two men was carrying a body. He was carrying it over his shoulder, like one would carry a sack of potatoes. As the images faded into the woods, Lila wondered who the corpse could be and why these two men would even be in there. Everything about this seemed highly unusual.

It took a long time before Lila was able to sleep that night as she tried to think about what to do next. No one in the asylum seemed to be trustworthy, so telling another nurse or Mr. Potter about what she had seen in the basement was out of the question. A few hours before the sun came up, Lila finally fell into a deep sleep and her mother entered her dreams again. This time she spoke, telling Lila, "Stay safe, my child, I am with you." Her words were comforting, but when Lila asked her what she should do, Amelia suddenly disappeared.

Just as Lila was waking up the next morning, she heard the sound of a male voice calling to her. "Good day, Miss Fern," it said cheerfully.

Lila opened her eyes and replied, "Oh, good morning, Doctor Asher."

"Is it okay if we have a short conversation?"

Lila, still shaken from the night before, responded, "Yes, of course, but what is this about?"

"It's been five days since you arrived at Hillside and I just wanted to see how you were doing."

Lila noticed Nurse Margaret standing in the doorway. Just seeing her made her nervous but she didn't let on and replied, "I think I am doing all right, it's just all new to me and I need time to adjust."

Doctor Asher then handed Lila a tablet and said, "This medication will help you feel much better and I suspect you will be back to your old self very soon."

Lila reluctantly did as he asked, swallowing this unknown tablet, all the while having Nurse Margaret standing over her and watching closely to make sure she did. Lila wasn't sure what she had swallowed, the tablet tasted bitter and stuck in her throat.

Doctor Asher then said, "I will give this medication to the nurse and she will administer it twice a day, it is proven to alleviate symptoms of depression."

With that, they both turn around and walked out the door. Right after they left, Lila stuck her finger down her throat hoping to cough up the tablet, but it was too late. Within an hour of taking it, she began to feel strange and very drowsy. Her memories of the next twelve hours were sketchy at best, but she did recall Nurse Margaret giving her another tablet later that night. Lila didn't know how much time had passed, but when she awoke Nurse Fiona was standing over her.

This time the nurse gave Lila her tablet and left the room without watching if she took it. As soon as she was out of sight, Lila spat it into the trash bin. After splashing some cold water on her face, she went down to see if Patty had returned to her room. She was there, but when she saw her, she couldn't believe her eyes. Patty's head was completely shaved and a bloody gauze dressing sat across her forehead. April was just staring at her in disbelief and told Lila, "She hasn't moved since they brought her back. I am so worried about her, do you think she's going to die?"

Lila leaned over Patty to make sure she was still breathing and noticed her hand twitching. She wondered out loud how much more Patty could take before she would succumb to the torture at Hillside. Lila believed that her only saving grace was her age, had she been older, surely her body would have given up by now. Lila didn't know what to tell April, who was now crying. To say that Patty would survive was premature, instead she simply said that she was worried too. The sooner she was transferred out of Hillside the better, but for now, all she could do was pray for her. The plan to move her was in motion and Lila knew Loraine would not let her down.

Later that same evening, Lila planned to speak to Josiah to see if he could provide her with a key that would open the doors in the cellar. In the meantime, she wrote a lengthy letter to Loraine, outlining what she had seen so far and urging her to pass her letter on to Billy. Lila feared the tablets she was taking would interfere with her investigation and she decided she would hide them under her tongue when Nurse Margaret was in and pretend to swallow. Lila found out that it was surprisingly easy to fool the nurses into believing she was taking them. Whatever they had been giving her had made her feel dizzy and extremely tired. Now, with a clear head, she stayed awake, waiting for Josiah to arrive.

Two hours after his shift ended, he hadn't arrived and Lila couldn't keep her eyes open any longer and drifted off to sleep. Josiah never did show up that night and Lila was getting worried. Without the ability to communicate with Loraine, her whole plan might backfire.

Back in Elmvale, Loraine was also concerned because she hadn't received any notes from Lila in several days. Now she wondered if Josiah had been caught. Loraine had no other choice but to make a visit to the asylum and demand to see her friend. Without Josiah, she had no way to make sure that Lila was safe. With this in mind, she went straight over to speak to Billy; she had to let him know what her plans were.

Loraine was feeling so frazzled that morning that she neglected to get a gift for his toy drive. Billy could see that she looked very worried and waved her into his office. As soon as she told him she had not received any further communication from Lila, he too became concerned. Hillside had such a bad reputation that he quickly agreed that Loraine should make an immediate visit to Hillside. In the meantime, he promised to get as much information as he could about Josiah and although he didn't have a last name for this boy, he did have connections all over town. If they could find Josiah, they would find out why he'd stopped delivering Lila's messages. Loraine planned on visiting Hillside the following day, hoping they would agree to let her see Lila. She also decided that until she knew exactly what was going on, she would not involve Elise or Mavis; she didn't want them to worry needlessly.

With no way to get the keys to unlock the doors in the cellar, Lila waited until the following night to venture back downstairs. She stole one of Nurse Daisy's hairpins, hoping she could jimmy the locks and get inside one of the rooms. She was cautiously optimistic this would work.

Just before midnight and with no sign of any of the staff, Lila took her lantern and quickly made her way through the corridor that led to the cellar stairs. Each step she took gave her a wave of anxiety, but she was determined to find out if Lois was still alive. Once she got downstairs, her heart began to race as she tried the first door, but the hairpin just bent inside the lock and it took her several minutes to get it out. When she tried the next door, to her surprise, it slowly opened. Feeling nervous about going inside she stopped and listened to make sure that no one had followed her there. It was pitch black inside the room, but as she shone her lantern from left to right, she was startled by an object on a gurney just inside the door. It looked like a body covered by a white sheet. Nervous, but determined to see who it was, she gently lifted the sheet and uncovered Lois's body. The elderly woman had two holes drilled into the side of her head, a trickle of dried blood lay under her nose and mouth. Lila was so frightened by the sight that she quickly turned away only to see another corpse laying nearby. After taking a deep breath and asking God for strength, Lila removed the sheet and saw another woman. This time, she had no idea who she was. Like Lois, she also had two holes drilled into her head, but unlike Lois, she had a rubber bar protruding from her mouth. Lila suddenly realized it was the same type of bar they had given her to bite on when she had the electric shock treatments.

Lila stood outside the room to calm herself down and gather her thoughts. She knew that she had to get as much information as possible that night, just in case she couldn't safely get down there again. Once she got her nerve to go back inside, she noticed a notepad sitting on a table beside the unknown victim. Lila held her lantern over it, but the writing wasn't very clear. After blowing the dust away, she made out the words "Constantine Rice, age 44, no family ties."

Now more of this bizarre mystery was coming together and beginning to make sense. It seemed that experiments were being done on patients that were considered abandoned by their loved ones. No one would ever come looking for these women.

Lila was done, she had seen enough for one night and now she had proof that something evil was happening at Hillside Asylum. Thankfully, she was able to get back to her room unnoticed, but she would have another restless night. As she lay in bed that night, Lila couldn't stop thinking about the two unfortunate souls she had seen in the cellar. Despite every effort to relax, Lila was still unable to sleep. It was a hot, humid night and she hoped that she could cool down by sitting near the window. The full moon lit up the night sky and she was able to write down everything she had seen in the hope that Josiah would return soon. Lila circled the name Constantine Rice and concluded that once she got out of Hillside, she would turn her information over to the constabulary with the hope that everyone involved with the torture and murder of these innocent people would pay the ultimate price.

It was nearly 4am when Lila once again heard screaming coming from the cellar. She knew in her heart that another poor soul was being tortured at the hands of those that were supposed to be looking after them. These horrific screams persisted for several minutes, but Lila also knew there was nothing she could do to help them. As she peered down the dark hallway she watched as Mildred Richards wandered back and forth, aimlessly searching for her home. She clutched a rag doll in her arms, as if it were her child. Her hands shook from too many electric shock treatments and although she walked right past Lila, she didn't seem to notice her. Lila felt she was one of the lucky ones, she had no idea what was going on and she didn't seem to care.

∼

The next day, Loraine was up very early and went straight to the asylum. She hoped that if she arrived before 8am that she would be able to speak directly to Mr. Potter and convince him that she needed to speak to her sister urgently. Loraine looked up at this imposing place after securing her horse and buggy to a fence post. Nervous, but determined, she walked right past the gardener who had left the gate open and straight into the front doors. It wasn't until she attempted to walk towards Lila's room that she was stopped by two orderlies, who insisted she had to leave immediately. Loraine stood her ground and screamed at them to unhand her, but her demands were ignored. They then forcibly led her to the front door and told her in no uncertain terms that she was not to return until the fifteenth of the month. As she walked away from the building feeling extremely frustrated, she heard one of the orderly's yell at the gardener for leaving the gate unlocked. Loraine didn't give up and instead of heading home she snuck around the back, hoping to catch a glimpse of Lila that morning. Unfortunately, she had forgotten to hide her horse and carriage. Loraine hoped that no one would notice as she peered through the windows above her. Unable to see very clearly, Loraine dragged an old crate over and stood on it, hoping this would allow her a better view into Hillside. A few seconds later, she was startled by someone tapping her shoulder. To her relief, she saw that it was the gardener, an older gentleman with a friendly smile. He had seen her come around to the back and wanted to warn her: "Please, Miss, go before anyone sees you. This place isn't safe and people seem to go missing all the time from here."

Loraine wanted to know more, but he insisted she leave right away and he pointed to an opening where she could sneak out and not be seen by anyone. As she hurried into the bush, she tripped on a spade that had been left there earlier. The earth beneath her was very soft and it looked much like a grave had been dug recently. Further into the bush, she found more disturbed soil. Loraine was so curious now that she began digging with her hands. In less than a foot of soil, she uncovered two tiny boxes, each containing the remains of infants not more than a day old. Loraine began to cry when she noticed that the tiny female infant still had its umbilical cord attached. This was the last thing she expected to uncover, and Loraine's whole body trembled as she carefully replaced these tiny boxes back into their unmarked graves.

Fear soon took over and Loraine suddenly became disoriented, unsure now what direction she needed to go in in order to get back to her carriage. She tried to calm herself down and as she stood looking down at the ground that held the bodies of two babies, she began to cry. How could this be? Why would these two innocent infants be buried behind an asylum? A few minutes later, Loraine was startled by the sound of someone coming towards her. Unsure where to go, she began to run, hoping she was going in the right direction. It wasn't long before she realized she was lost, which only increased her anxiety further. Now out of breath and filled with apprehension, she hid behind a tree to rest. Once Loraine was able to calm herself down, she briefly considered returning to the graves to retrieve the infants. Although she was angry with herself for not taking them when she had a chance, she knew she might put Lila in harm's way if she attempted to go back.

It took another hour before Loraine found her way back to her carriage. By this time, she was feeling very irritable. Her arms and face were covered in mosquito bites and she was dealing with heat exhaustion. A routine visit to see her friend had backfired horribly and exposed even more of the secrets that Hillside held. As Loraine sat inside her carriage looking up at the asylum, she saw someone looking at her from an upstairs window. Loraine could not make out the woman's face but noticed she was wearing a white smock and cap and realized right away it was one of the nurses. Feeling unnerved and confused by what she had seen, she raced back to Elmvale to speak to Billy.

Once there, Loraine began to feel safe again but as she took her horse into the stables, she noticed a man watching her; it was the orderly she had seen at Hillside, the one that had insisted she leave. Loraine knew that this wasn't a coincidence and decided to go into the mercantile, hoping he would be gone by the time she came out. As she busied herself shopping for a toy, she watched out the window until she was sure he was no longer there. She certainly did not want him knowing she was meeting with Billy and when she felt it was safe to leave, she snuck out with a few other shoppers and went directly to the *Examiner*. Loraine was so determined to talk to Billy that she hadn't even noticed the dirt on her knees or dress. It wasn't until his secretary asked if she had fallen that she realized why some of the women inside the mercantile were staring at her. The minute Billy saw her he took a bottle of whiskey from his drawer and poured them each a large drink. Loraine told him to take notes as she explained everything that had happened that morning. Billy was so concerned now for both her safety as well as Lila's that he told her not to go back until they went together on the fifteenth of the month.

Loraine realized that it had been a mistake to go to Hillside that morning, and now fearing that she may have made things worse for Lila, she promised Billy she would wait. Thankfully, Billy did have some good news for her, he had located the address where Josiah lived and planned on making a visit to his home after work that day. He said he lived five miles east of town and invited Loraine along, so she could talk to him personally.

After a couple of drinks with Billy, Loraine was able to relax a little and went back to her hotel to bathe and change into some clean clothes. Billy had made extensive notes and even drew a map outlining where Loraine had said the two infants were buried. He did not want to forget anything she told him about her visit that morning. The more he knew about Hillside the better. Billy had always believed the rumours about this asylum, but he was never able to prove that any wrongdoing had occurred there. Mr. Potter always had a team of expensive lawyers that quashed all charges ever filed against him. Billy hoped this time would be different, but he was aware that if anyone found out what they were up to, they would find a way to hide any evidence before it could be discovered.

Now that Loraine had bathed and changed into clean clothes, she was ready to face the rest of the day. She was desperate to learn how Lila was doing and she hoped that Josiah would have some answers for her. Billy was also anxious to find out what was going on and, on the way, he told Loraine that he would not leave until he got the truth.

Josiah's home was nothing more than a one room wooden shack and it gave him little shelter from the elements. As Billy approached the front porch, he could hear someone moving inside. He had never met Josiah and wasn't even sure if it was him. When the young man came to the door Billy said, "I am looking for Josiah, could that be you, sir?"

Josiah said, "Yes, and who are you?" Billy didn't say he was a reporter, instead he said he was a friend of Loraine Powel and her sister Lila. As soon as he mentioned her name, Josiah slammed the door in his face.

Billy called in, "I just have a few questions about Lila, and I won't leave until I get some answers!"

When Loraine came onto the porch she banged on the door and told Josiah that it was urgent they speak with him.

A few minutes later, he opened the door and said, "Please just leave, if Mr. Potter finds out you were here, he will foreclose on my house and this is all I have left."

Loraine said, "We'll leave as soon as you answer a few questions, please just tell me if Lila is okay?"

Josiah looked around to make sure no one else was nearby and replied, "The last time 1 saw her she was recovering from electric shock treatment, now hurry, please go."

Loraine had much more to say but he slammed the door again and refused to open it. It was obvious someone had learned about Loraine's messages to Lila and possibly Lila's message to her. This wasn't good and they both knew it. Now Loraine was filled with remorse and worry. If only she had talked Lila out of this, if only she had stopped her from entering Hillside in the first place.

11

It was difficult to hear that Lila had endured electric shock treatments and this worried Loraine and Billy. They knew that she was of sound mind and wondered why on earth a doctor would have put her through such an invasive procedure. Billy knew that it was an overused practice in these places and hoped Lila was strong enough to endure the treatments, and he prayed that this would all be over soon.

Loraine was frightened by what she had heard and despite Lila's insistence that she was fine, she was now considering the option of moving her out of there sooner than they had planned. Loraine and Lila had discussed the dangers, but neither of them were prepared for this. Loraine told Billy that Lila made light of it all and promised she would be just fine, now she wasn't so sure. Billy was also concerned and told Loraine that he would visit Josiah the following day and pressure him into divulging what had happened.

Feeling uneasy and unsure as to what she was going to say to Elise and Mavis, Loraine reluctantly went to their home to give them an update. When she arrived a short time later, Elise came running out to greet her. Within a few seconds she instinctively knew by the look on Loraine's face, that something was terribly wrong. Loraine had no other choice but to lie, as she did her best to skirt the truth and put her mind at ease. Although she felt that she had been convincing, Elise later told Mavis that she didn't believe Loraine was being forthcoming.

After a brief and somewhat uncomfortable visit, Loraine left and returned to her hotel. Her mind was racing as she passed by the clerk and headed up to her room. She just couldn't get the images of the infants she had seen in the woods beside Hillside out of her thoughts and did not hear the clerk asking her twice for a moment of her time. A few minutes after she arrived in her room the clerk knocked on her door. Loraine had had a visitor that day, someone the clerk described as being "confrontational". She described what he looked like to Loraine and then said, "This man was rather pushy and he asked several times if he could wait inside your room for your return. I explained this was against our policy and after he angrily slammed his fist on my desk, I insisted he leave."

The visitor's description sounded very much like the same orderly she saw the previous day. Loraine had no idea why he had been there and no idea why he was insisting on speaking to her now. Feeling somewhat concerned for her own safety, she asked that if he returned to tell him that she had left Elmvale and was travelling back home.

Although Loraine was a strong, independent woman, she couldn't help feeling vulnerable at times. She had experienced a lot of verbal threats in her days as a suffragette, but never once worried about physical harm. This was altogether different and the visit from the same orderly that insisted she leave Hillside really frightened her. As she sat by her window, watching and waiting to see if he returned, thoughts of her husband Ernest entered her mind. He had returned to London to take care of some business shortly after Lila was admitted to Hillside and now she wished with all her heart that he was there by her side.

After spending less than two weeks in Hillside, Lila became increasingly suspicious of Nurse Margaret's behaviour. Throughout her stay, Nurse Margaret had been short-tempered with her, abrupt and forceful at times, even going so far as insisting the doctor give her shock treatments. In spite of all those things, that morning she was acting totally different. For the first time since Lila arrived at Hillside, Nurse Margaret was being pleasant to her. She smiled when she greeted her that morning and even offered her a clean frock and fresh linens for her bed. According to Gladys and Esther, this was unheard of, they only received a fresh frock on the fourteenth of the month and their beds were rarely changed. Lila later listened at her door as Nurse Margaret made her rounds. She could clearly hear her chastising April for wetting her bed again and screaming at another patient for getting in her way. Lila was extremely angry at her for the nasty comments she made to April and after she left the floor that morning, she went directly to her room.

As suspected, April was in bits and it took Lila several minutes to calm her down. Sadly, Patty's condition had not changed and she was still in the same position she had left her in. April did say that her eyes had opened a few times and that Doctor Asher had held her up and given her some medicine and a few sips of water. Lila asked, "Has she spoken or cried out in pain?"

April replied, "Not a word, but she did moan in her sleep last night."

Lila sat by Patty's side, brushing the hair away from her face as she whispered, "Don't you worry now; I promise that you will be out of this place very soon."

April asked Lila again if she really was going to help her as well as Patty. Lila confirmed that she would. She could not walk away from this young girl now and she knew that if her mother was alive that she would be doing the exact same thing. No one, not even the doctors, had done what they promised April's mother they would do. April was left in her bed day and night and only taken out for meals. This was not supposed to happen. Lila, albeit somewhat prematurely, had made April a promise and she knew that when she left Hillside that she would have to find alternate arrangements for her too. She was very intelligent and could easily function on her own with just a little help with her daily needs. April missed her mother terribly and had told Lila that she was worried about her. April had not received one letter or visit since her arrival and this was completely out of character.

Lila, who had no ties with April before Hillside, promised she would also speak to her mother once she was released. Her kindness and willingness to help anyone in need was in her very nature. She was so much like her own mother, Amelia, who would never have turned her back on anyone. Lila knew that if she was alive today, she would be doing everything in her power to help both Patty and April.

Lila stayed with Patty until she heard Doctor Asher's familiar voice coming towards her. When she returned to her room, Doctor Asher was already there. It seemed he wanted to see if the medication he had prescribed was helping her symptoms. He was also surprised to hear that she was as active as she was, since this particular drug normally caused excessive drowsiness.

After a brief discussion, Doctor Asher concluded that the medication was working and he promised to reduce it to one tablet a day if Lila's symptoms continued to improve. Like Nurse

Margaret had that morning, he too seemed to be treating her differently and although he had a gentle bedside manner, his visits were usually brief and to the point. Lila wasn't falling for his boyish smile and gentle manner because lurking behind that smile was a man capable of unimaginable acts of cruelty. He was experimenting on patients who couldn't resist, ones without family or friends to protect them. Now believing that he would have to eventually answer for his crimes against humanity, Lila played the role of a naïve patient very well.

As the days passed without any relevant improvement in Patty's condition, Lila couldn't wait for Loraine to visit. She had so much to tell her about Hillside and she was desperate to find out when Patty would be transferred. Lila knew that if it wasn't soon that she might die. Nurse Fiona was also concerned about Patty, yet nothing more was done for her. Lila knew there was an infirmary in the asylum and when she asked why Patty hadn't been moved there, Nurse Fiona didn't have the answer. All she said was, "You know, Lila, I've asked myself that same question, I have even notified the doctors, yet here she is, clinging on to life by a thread." Lila trusted this nurse; she was different and she seemed to actually care about the patients at Hillside. She also knew that Nurse Fiona would lose her job if she dared to question Doctor Asher's orders or any other doctor at Hillside.

Visiting day was getting closer and Lila wondered if Isaac would come in to see her. They had exchanged harsh words about her decision to enter Hillside the last time they spoke, but she hoped that he had come to terms with it and now understood her motivation for wanting to do this. As she thought about her own mother's sacrifice, Lila knew that despite her husband's misgivings, she had done the right thing. Isaac's last words resonated within her: "Come on, Lila, be reasonable, your place is here, with me and Isabel and we should be your priority, not some young woman that you barely know!"

This had not only angered Lila, it would forever change the way she looked at her husband. Had she listened to him, Patty, April and so many others that were trapped inside Hillside, tortured inside this dreadful place, would never have a voice.

Lila spent the rest of the day compiling notes about Hillside and its staff. This itemized list was carefully hidden under her mattress and only Gladys and Esther knew it was there.

Back at home, Billy had finally received some good news. Chris Miller had been located in Thornberry and would be in front of a judge the following month. In the meantime, he would now feel like a caged animal as he was sat inside a six-by-three-foot cell, his freedom a distant past. Just knowing he was there brought some joy into Loraine's life and she couldn't wait to share this news with Lila.

With Chris finally where he belonged, Billy decided it was time to pay another visit to Josiah. He hoped he could learn more about Lila's condition and why he had suddenly stopped passing Loraine's notes to her. Billy would wait until dark before going back to see him, he wanted to make sure no one was around when he arrived.

It had rained most of the day and as soon as he got thirty feet from Josiah's property, the wheels on Billy's carriage got stuck in the mud. Still hoping no one had heard him arrive, he quietly approached Josiah's shack. The minute he got onto the porch he heard Josiah and another man arguing. Unsure who he would face if he knocked on the door, he decided to hide beneath the front window and listen. The man arguing with Josiah had an arrogance about him and Billy knew right away that it was none other than Mr. Andrew Potter.

He had met him the previous year, when he'd covered a case involving a young girl who had become pregnant whilst in his care at Hillside. Billy couldn't make out everything they were saying, but he did hear Mr. Potter threaten Josiah, telling him, "I don't know what Loraine Powel is up to, but no one crosses me and if I find out you were involved in any way, I will burn this house down with you in it!" Josiah had a somewhat meek response to his acquisitions, "I don't know anything, sir, only that she wanted me to pass notes back and forth between her and Lila Fern."

Billy felt a little sorry for the young lad and now understood why he initially refused to talk to them. At this time, he decided not to make matters worse for him and returned to his home in Elmvale. On the way back, he stopped at Loraine's hotel to let her know what he had heard. Loraine agreed with Billy, Josiah was just another pawn in Mr. Potter's life, someone easily replaceable in his eyes.

With just two days left before visiting day at Hillside, Billy learned that Casandra Miller had given birth to a baby girl. Sadly, Casandra was still very much in love with Chris and sent her sister with the bail money needed for his release. She desperately wanted Chris to see the beautiful baby girl they had created but to her dismay, his bail was denied. Casandra apparently was heartbroken; she had believed all the horrible lies that Chris had told her about Patty. He had said that Ian wasn't even his child and that Patty had fooled him into believing that he was the father, only to force him into a loveless marriage. Disturbingly, Casandra would only hear what she wanted to hear, nothing anyone told her about Chris's past seemed to get through to her.

Billy was elated that Chris was behind bars, he had wanted to see justice for Patty and Ian for a very long time. He couldn't understand what would possess a man to turn his back on his disabled wife and helpless infant son and decided it was time to make a visit to the prison to see Chris himself.

Billy would later write in his notes: *I cannot believe the garbage that spewed out of Chris Miller's mouth. His only excuse for leaving Patty was because he was bored with her and she couldn't satisfy his marital needs any longer. He later bragged about the women in his life and how he once had an affair with a married woman who was ten years older than him and much more experienced. When I asked, "Do you not care that your wife will suffer for what you did for the rest of her life?" Chris smiled and said, "Patty will get over it eventually, besides, now she doesn't have to look after a screaming baby all day so I guess in the long run we all win."* His response shocked Billy who thought he had seen and heard everything.

Chris, it seemed, was absolutely immune to others' suffering and even when Billy mentioned the birth of his second child, all he was concerned about was Casandra's figure, telling Billy, "I sure hope her condition didn't turn her into another fat fish-wife." Throughout his interview with him, Chris did not ask how Casandra was feeling or how his baby daughter was doing. Chris was concerned about one person and that was himself. In the end, Billy left the prison feeling like he needed to shower. This self-absorbed, poor excuse for a man wanted something in return for granting this interview and when Chris asked that he do him a favour, Billy got up abruptly and left without respond-ing. All he could think about as he headed back to his office was why Patty was in an asylum and not him.

Chris had no idea at the time that Billy was planning on writing another scathing article about how his selfish acts had been directly responsible for the death of his infant son and his wife's mental breakdown. Billy never wanted his readers to forget about what Chris Miller had done. It would never bring back Ian or make Patty well again, but it would give Billy a way to expose him for the kind of low life scoundrel that he was.

Billy laughed when he told Loraine what a fool Chris was, he had passed a paper across to him and asked him to sign it. He said, "You know the moron didn't even read it?" This small victory would allow Billy all rights to his story without ever being charged with defamation of character. Although the reporters were given unwritten permission to write at will, Billy knew that at times he crossed a fine line. Chris, in turn, had such a big ego that he mistook his intentions, thinking Billy was going to write an article that made him look like some sort of a victim instead of the spoiled child that was hiding inside the body of a grown man.

Believing things were finally working in their favour, Loraine tried her best to stop worrying about her closest friend. She knew Lila was a strong and intelligent woman and one who would never take unnecessary risks. She also knew that if she suspected injustice in any shape or form that she would do whatever it took to bring this information to light.

Loraine would have another restless night as Audrey, the desk clerk, mentioned that the orderly from Hillside had been back asking for her again. Although she did as Loraine asked and told the man she had returned home, she felt that he wasn't convinced. Loraine didn't know why the orderly was following her but she also didn't want to risk finding out. Unable to sleep that night, Loraine decided it was time to call her husband. They hadn't spoken for several days and Ernest was thrilled to hear from her despite the late hour. He could tell by her tone that she wasn't herself and insisted before hanging up that he come to Elmvale to be with her. Loraine had always felt invincible and at first, she told him not to bother, but deep down she was extremely relieved to find out Ernest would soon be by her side.

After speaking to Ernest, Loraine was finally able to get some rest, but the very next morning, she awoke feeling anxious and the minute she opened her eyes, her thoughts turned to Lila.

~

Lila had slept late that morning and missed breakfast. She couldn't be certain, but she woke up so groggy that day that she thought someone might have put some sleeping powder into her tea the evening before. When she got out of bed, she had to hold on to the dresser to steady herself, something was wrong, but she had little recall of the night before. Once she splashed some cool water on her face, she realised that no one else was around. Having only been there a short while, she didn't know the routine that happened before visiting day of each month. It was on these days that all the patients were bathed and received a clean frock. Some even received clean bedding, depending on whether they were having visitors. Lila knew that this was only for show as during the rest of the month few were bathed and even fewer received clean clothing. Minutes later, Nurse Margaret came into her room and told Lila to follow her.

Lila asked, "Where are you taking me?"

Nurse Margaret smiled and then replied, "For a bath, of course."

Lila followed her into a room that she had never been in before. A large tub filled with water sat in the middle and she immediately noticed a wire dangling inside it. Lila turned to run away but an orderly came out of nowhere and forced her towards the tub. Lila screamed as loud as she could as Nurse Margaret forcefully stripped off her frock then pushed her into the electrically charged water. The moment she entered, Lila felt a current of electricity pass through her and then suddenly, the room went dark.

It seemed that Nurse Margaret had falsely accused Lila of poisoning the minds of some of Hillside's patients and with the nurse's insistence, her lover, Doctor Asher had ordered the hydrotherapy bath which included a small amount of electrical current to make her more co-operative and subdued. Lila did not remember returning to her room that day and when she woke up several hours later to the sound of the three bells, she knew it indicated that a meal was being served. She was surprised to hear that it was nearly five in the evening. Too weak to walk to the dining area she lay in bed, trying to remember what happened that day.

All evening she fell in out of sleep and just before morning she had a terrible dream that she was being electrocuted. Just as she awoke, everything came rushing back to her and she vividly remembered being dragged into the bath after being stripped of her clothing by Nurse Margaret. She hadn't seen Doctor Asher, but recalled hearing his voice just before being put back into her bed. As Lila tried to sit up, she noticed burn marks on her left arm and recalled seeing the same marks on Patty's arms.

No one else was around when Nurse Margaret came into her room early the next morning. She seemed to enjoy watching Lila struggle as she stood in the doorway after ordering her to get up out of bed. Lila just didn't have the strength or the will to leave her room, but Nurse Margaret insisted and brought in two orderlies that forced her up, then dragged her down the hallway and into the dining room. Once they left, Lila leaned up against the wall praying she wouldn't fall on the filthy floor below her.

The room was spinning, and she felt like she would vomit at any moment when suddenly, a patient she had never seen before came within inches of her face and screamed obscenities in her ear. It startled Lila so much that she did end up falling to the floor. As she lay there moaning in pain, no one bothered to help her, some even stepped on her as they left the dining area. Lila would remain there for over two hours before Nurse

Margaret would allow anyone to help her back to her room. She had warned the other patients to stay away from her or risk going to the Preston Wing. No one dared touch Lila and although some wanted to, including Gladys and Esther, they knew Nurse Margaret would make their lives a living hell.

By this time, Lila was barely conscious, but she could feel a sharp, stabbing pain radiating up her leg. Lila tried to focus on her surroundings as she was being dragged back to her room but she still felt dizzy and disoriented from the previous treatment she had endured. Her left leg was twisted behind her and she screamed out in agony as the attendants paid little attention to her cries.

Tossed onto her bed without any regard for her injuries, she looked up to see Nurse Margaret smiling down at her. Lila was shocked by how she had been treated and despite her fear and the pain she was in, she looked directly into Nurse Margaret's eyes and said, "You will regret this, you sick, twisted, wicked woman, I will make sure of that!"

Nurse Margaret smiled, then glared at Lila before telling the orderlies to leave. A few seconds later she leaned directly on her injured leg and whispered, "You, Miss Fern, won't be alive long enough to do anything to me!"

This caused Lila to scream out again. The pain was unbearable and she could see that Nurse Margaret was enjoying every minute of it.

12

Nurse Fiona was summoned by Gladys the minute she came into work that evening. Lila had been crying out all day and no one, not even the doctor, had come in to check on her. Gladys was worried; she had never seen her in such pain, and she told Nurse Fiona that the bone on her leg was protruding out of the skin. Nurse Fiona was dealing with another emergency and couldn't come straight away but she promised she would be there as soon as she could.

Fifteen minutes later she arrived to see that Gladys wasn't imagining things, Lila's leg was certainly fractured and it was twice the size of the uninjured one. Without any further hesitation, she immediately had her patient transferred to the infirmary. Once Lila was as comfortable as she could possibly be, Nurse Fiona went back to see if Nurse Margaret had charted anything about this. To her surprise, she had neglected to indicate her injuries in her nursing notes even though Gladys had mentioned that it was Nurse Margaret that had brought Lila back to her bed. At this point, Nurse Fiona had no idea what had happened to Lila. Nurse Margaret's last notation indicated that Lila had an electric bath therapy and nothing more.

Later that evening, Nurse Fiona would learn the truth. Nurse Margaret had left Lila on the floor in the dining area after she fell and didn't attend to her for almost two hours. This was unacceptable and everyone who witnessed Lila's suffering knew it. Nurse Fiona knew that she couldn't possibly let this go unnoticed. Nurse Margaret had done some questionable things in the past, only some of which Nurse Fiona was aware of, but this seemed outright cruel. To make sure that this was documented, she purposely wrote a lengthy report indicating everything that had happened, naming Nurse Margaret as having "blatantly disregarded the needs of her patient". Afterwards and before leaving that night, she went to the infirmary to check on Lila.

She was sleeping, having been given pain medication the moment she arrived in the infirmary. Although her pain was being managed, she still had a long recovery ahead of her. Doctor Jerome told Nurse Fiona that the injury would heal in time, but he was concerned that she would end up with a noticeable limp because he did not have an operating theatre and was only able to reset the fracture by manual alignment. The doctor was also concerned about Lila's overall health, she was extremely thin and very dehydrated. Burn marks to her wrists and her partially shaved head indicated that she had received several, probably unnecessary, procedures prior to arriving at the infirmary, which was located near the patient records, in the east side of the basement. This was also a concern and might play a role in her recovery.

Doctor Jerome had only been working at Hillside for about six weeks and already he voiced concerns to Nurse Fiona about the conditions there. Unfortunately, she had seen many doctors come and go and now she was concerned that he would be the next. He was not a psychiatrist like the others, but he did understand the illnesses of the mind. Nurse Fiona had faith in this doctor, he was different from the others and like her, he seemed to care about his patients.

With a plan to speak to Mr. Potter about Nurse Margaret the following day, she left feeling that Lila was in the best hands and the best place for her recovery.

The next morning, as planned, Nurse Fiona arrived early to speak to Mr. Potter. Surely, he couldn't ignore her this time. As she anxiously waited, she took her notes from her pocket and went over what she was going to say. Mr. Potter was always in a rush and she knew he would only allow her a few minutes of his time.

Just prior to being called into his office, Nurse Margaret came by and whispered in her ear, "You know you're wasting your time; I've got Andrew exactly where I want him and nothing you say will make a bit of difference."

Nurse Fiona didn't respond and although she had no idea what she meant; she took her comment with a grain of salt.

An hour later, Nurse Fiona was called into his office. Mr. Potter felt that nurses were there for his convenience, nothing more and was irritated to hear that she wanted to file a complaint. As she entered his office, he seemed agitated and somewhat distracted. Before Nurse Fiona could say a word, he said, "My time is valuable, please do not waste it on trivial matters."

Now feeling extremely nervous, she stuttered as she spoke about her concerns regarding Nurse Margaret, Lila Fern's fracture, and she also mentioned the unorthodox methods Doctor Asher was using on patients.

After she was finished, Mr. Potter looked up from his desk, his face was red and twisted and without warning he slammed his notepad down and said, "It is none of your business what methods our fine doctors use here! You are merely his servant, nothing more, and I suggest you start looking for another job because as of this moment your services are no longer needed at Hillside!"

Nurse Fiona didn't know what to say, he had no reason to fire her, she was simply doing her job.

Back in Elmvale, Ernest arrived as expected and Loraine was so happy to see him, she practically leaped into his arms. As they headed over to pick up Billy, she explained everything that was happening at the asylum and how she had stumbled across the two tiny graves in the woods.

Nervously awaiting her first visit with Lila, Loraine didn't stop talking all the way to the asylum. Billy was nervous too and did his best to disguise himself, but his long white beard still remained a rather prominent part of his face. Still, he hoped he wouldn't be recognized that day. When they finally arrived at Hillside, they noticed a long line-up of family and friends anxious to see their loved ones.

Lila had mentioned this to Loraine and for that reason, it didn't surprise her. Some travelled for several miles just to have an hour with their loved ones. It took almost forty-five minutes, standing outside on this very hot and humid day, for them to reach the front of the line, but the minute they mentioned Lila's name, they were stopped from going inside. An orderly told Loraine that Lila had fallen and was now in the infirmary and that absolutely no guests were allowed inside there. Billy and Ernest were not satisfied with his explanation and insisted on seeing Lila before they left.

Billy said, "For God's sake, son, you can see that her sister is upset, I'm sure a five-minute visit wouldn't hurt anyone."

Loraine was crying, which made Ernest more determined

and he demanded to speak to Mr. Potter. He told the orderly in a rather loud, formidable voice, "We have no intentions of leaving this place until we see Lila, now move out of our damn way!"

Billy had had enough and pushed his way past the two orderlies who were blocking the main door as Ernest and Loraine followed close behind. Once inside, all three went directly to Mr. Potter's office, who was on the phone as they all barged in.

"What the hell is going on here!" Andrew Potter demanded.

Ernest was the first to speak up. "Today is visiting day, is it not?" Before Mr. Potter could answer he added, "We are here to see my sister-in-law, Lila Fern, and I suggest you tell us where we can find her."

Mr. Potter stood and pointed to the door. "Leave at this moment, or I will have to call the constable."

Billy walked right over to Mr. Potter, his sheer size was enough to intimidate anyone and as he looked down at him, he said, "Why don't you just do that? I cannot wait to expose you and the horrific living conditions in this place."

Mr. Potter realized who Billy was and as he backed away from him, he said, "You, Mr. Carter, are not welcome here, now leave or I will have you arrested."

By now Ernest was so angry that his face had turned bright red and the veins in his neck began to protrude. He had had enough of Mr. Potter's smug attitude and shouted, "Do you have any idea who I am? I can have this place closed down by the month's end if you do not let us see Lila this minute!"

Andrew Potter didn't say a word as he walked towards the filing cabinet beside his desk. A few minutes later, he sat back down and threw the contract between Loraine Powel on behalf of Lila Fern directly at Ernest and said, "I suggest you read paragraph eight, line three."

Ernest took out his spectacles and found the paragraph. In

fine print it read: *Patients admitted to the infirmary for any reason, shall not receive visitors until such a patient has made a full recovery.* Ernest read it then leaned towards Mr. Potter and said, "You, sir, have not heard the last of this. I will be back in the morning with my lawyer!"

Loraine had been crying the entire time and when Ernest led her out of the asylum, she said to him, "What if she's dead, what if they have already killed her?"

Ernest assured her that Lila was alive and told her that he would get to the bottom of this within a few days.

Billy's usually light-hearted demeanour had vanished entirely, and as they walked out of the building, he punched the wall, leaving a hole as large as his fist in the plaster.

Mr. Potter didn't seem concerned by their threats, but yelled at Billy for damaging the wall. "I will be seeking the funds to repair the damage you caused, Mr. Carter, now be sure to bring your cheque book next time you come in."

Billy turned to confront him, but he had already gone back into his office.

As they walked down the narrow path leading to their wagon, Ernest saw two of the orderlies carrying what looked like a body wrapped in a sheet out the side door. Not wanting to upset Loraine any further, he did not mention this to her. Now curious about what they were carrying he asked that Billy accompany him around the back, telling Loraine that he just wanted to have a quick look around before they headed home.

As Loraine sat in the carriage trying to compose herself, Ernest told Billy what he had seen as they snuck around the back, hoping to catch up to the men before they disappeared into the woods. Unfortunately, they were not fast enough and when they got to the entrance of the wooded area, they couldn't see them anywhere. Ernest was so concerned by the sight and

Mr. Potter's attitude that he went straight back to the hotel and made several phone calls. One to a private detective, the other call was made to a lawyer in London. It would take another two days before they would arrive in Elmvale. Although Loraine was meant to give Elise and Mavis updates at this time, she didn't have the heart to tell them that she had been unable to see Lila or what was going on at Hillside. She knew that the blame would fall on her shoulders if anything happened to Lila.

During a conversation in Loraine's hotel room the next day, Billy proposed a plan that might just work to expose Andrew Potter and all of the asylum's secrets, but he also mentioned that it could be dangerous. Ernest was open to anything that may result in having this place shut down for good.

Billy told Ernest that one of his employees was a professional photographer and that he was willing to document everything on film, including taking photos of the remains of the infants found in the woods.

Billy said, "If we don't get there soon there is a likelihood that Mr. Potter will move the bodies to hide any evidence of wrongdoing. You know as well as l do that the pitiful excuse for a man needs to be stopped in his tracks, but once you bring a lawyer in, he will do whatever it takes to disprove our accusations, including getting rid of any evidence, just like he did the last time he was brought before the Crown."

Ernest agreed that it was a good idea but thought his private investigator should be the one to uncover any evidence.

Billy added, "There is no time to waste and no guarantee that the bodies will still be there when he arrives." With that said, all three decided to go ahead with the plan and to seal the deal, they had a few shots of whiskey before heading out to pick up the photographer.

Jacob O'Reilly was the best photographer Billy had ever

hired, and he had absolutely no fear. He told Ernest that one time when a bar brawl broke out at the Winchester Arms, he got in the middle of it all and began taking photos so everyone would know who the perpetrators were. Billy had already spoken to Jacob and told him exactly what he would be taking photos of and without hesitation, he agreed to do it.

Back at Hillside, Mr. Potter was said to be in a foul mood and had spent half the morning locked inside his office with his lawyers. It was clear to everyone that worked there that he was outraged by Ernest's remarks the day before.

In the meantime, Nurse Margaret had been heard bragging about having Nurse Fiona fired. April had overheard her telling an orderly that she could get away with anything at Hillside and never have to worry about losing her job.

Inside the infirmary, Lila was one of three patients. The pain had subsided substantially, but Lila was far too weak to even hold up her head to have a drink of water. Now in a place that was relatively safe, she would eventually regain her strength.

Thankfully, Nurse Margaret had made no attempt to see her or follow up on her condition, but she did come across the notes Lila had written. The morning of her transfer into the infirmary, her mattress shifted, exposing the notepads that Lila had hidden under it, but luckily she had written them in such a way that only she could understand the meaning behind them. Gladys was now terribly worried for Lila's safety; she had no idea that Lila had made sure that the notes wouldn't expose her and reveal the real reason why she had entered Hillside. Now in the wrong hands, Gladys feared Nurse Margaret would do much worse to Lila than she had already done.

As Billy, Ernest and Loraine made their way to the asylum that evening, they knew that the heat and humidity would play a role in what they would come across – the soaring temperatures would surely have had an effect on the rate of decomposition. Upon arrival, Billy quickly walked the horse and carriage into the woods, making sure that it was out of sight. He was determined to get what they came for and he told Jacob that it was imperative they get as much evidence as possible, even if they might be seen by the attendants.

Loraine who had seen the tiny coffins in the first place, nervously led the way. She remembered exactly where she had tripped over the spade and the approximate area where she had come across the remains of the infants.

No one lit their lantern until they were out of view and even though it was pitch black out there, they managed to find the first area Loraine had described.

Billy was the first to light his lantern and as soon as he did, he concluded that what they had found was in fact a grave. He then knelt down and told Jacob to start taking pictures. In the meantime, Loraine stood and watched the asylum, making sure no one had followed them.

Ernest and Billy took the discarded spade that was still sitting on the ground where it had been left and dug until they reached the body. Jacob took several more pictures as they removed the sheet from the corpse; it was an older woman with two holes, one on each side of her skull, visible.

Jacob got in as close as he could to take the photo, but the smell was overwhelming, and he began to gag and cough. Fearing he was making too much noise, he backed into the woods until his throat cleared. Once he was satisfied that he had taken enough photos, they carefully wrapped the body and placed her back into the ground. Loraine said a short prayer over her makeshift grave, before she led them to the two smaller graves.

It didn't take long to find the exact spot, there was still displaced soil from where she had been digging, and the two tiny boxes which contained their remains sat exactly where Loraine had left them. Billy removed the soil with his hands as Jacob took several photos. Once the infant's corpses were revealed, Loraine had to walk away. She was overcome with emotion and went to sit down nearby until she could calm herself. After they finished doing what they came for, they reluctantly placed the precious infants back into their boxes and buried them deeper into the ground, fearing they would be dragged off by an animal.

Once Billy exposed Hillside's secrets, he and Ernest planned to give all three corpses a proper burial. Now fearing there could be more, they walked around for a while and discovered one other grave, but this one hadn't been occupied. It appeared that it was still awaiting its next victim. Loraine was far too distraught to stay any longer, all she could think about was that this empty grave had been purposely dug to hold Lila's remains. No one could console her as they walked out of the woods.

Once safely inside their carriage they all noticed an orderly standing by the gate, he was about to smoke his pipe and when he lit a match, Loraine gasped. She knew this man; he had been the one following her.

Billy also recognized him; he had been arrested the previous year for vandalizing property when the owner had refused to hire him to build his barn. No one was really surprised he had a job at Hillside, Mr. Potter wasn't picky about who he hired, providing they did their job.

This night had been difficult, and all three were visibly upset by what they had seen. Loraine lay on Ernest's shoulder, her eyes red and swollen from crying. Billy took the reins as they slowly made their way back and he didn't say another word. Jacob and Ernest stared out into the darkness, both bewildered and disheartened by what they had discovered.

13

Doctor Jerome was surprised to see Nurse Margaret the following day. He had been expecting Fiona and was disappointed to see that she had not come into work. He didn't like Margaret one bit, and he also didn't trust her and watched as she pretended to to be compassionate towards Lila.

As she stood over her, she said, "Oh you poor dear, you have only been here such a short time and already you have suffered so. Now don't you worry, you will soon be as good as new."

Lila didn't move or even open her eyes, but she did hear exactly what Nurse Margaret had said. Lila then waited until she was certain she had left the room before speaking to the doctor. In a weak, barely audible voice, she said, "It was that nurse, she caused my injuries."

Doctor Jerome wasn't sure if he heard her correctly and asked, "Are you saying Nurse Margaret was responsible for your broken leg?"

Lila nodded, "Yes, and l think she is going to kill me."

Doctor Jerome wasn't as surprised as Lila thought he would be. He had already been told by Fiona and some of the other patients that Nurse Margaret had a quick temper and cruel streak. In fact, Frances Alderby, another patient inside the infirmary, had told him that she had been sent to the quiet room simply because she had asked for a clean frock.

Now burdened with this information, he wasn't sure what to do about it. He, like many doctors before him, had noticed some irregularities in the care given by certain staff members, specifically Nurse Margaret. He had also heard rumours of patients being forced to have shock treatments and Lila confirmed that this was true. Although he had recently been contemplating leaving his position there, he was not about to turn his back on this patient, not as long as he felt she could be in danger. Lila would later realize how lucky she was to have had him on her side.

Lila's purpose for entering Hillside was initially to oversee the care that Patty was receiving and to expose any deficiencies at the asylum. She never dreamed that she too would be the target of abuse and neglect. As she lay in the infirmary, she wondered if this had all been worth it. The pain from her fracture was causing a lot of discomfort and now she was beginning to feel defeated. She was also missing her baby daughter and her husband. For the first time since she arrived at Hillside, all she wanted to do was go home to her family.

It would take another spiritual visit from her mother to help her through this. As Lila fell in and out of a drug-induced sleep her mother, Amelia, came into her dreams. She looked like an angel as she stood at the edge of her bed. Her eyes were full of life, yet even in her dream-like state, Lila knew she was dead. As she floated around her, Lila tried desperately to reach out, but each time she appeared she just drifted away. Lila was desperate to hear what her mother would do in this circumstance and said, "Please, Mother, tell me if what I'm doing will make any difference, should I just leave Hillside and try and forget I was even here, or stay? I just don't know."

Amelia began to fade away, but just before she disappeared entirely, she said, "Life isn't always easy, dear, but I know in my heart that you will do what's right." Just then, Lila was awakened by Doctor Jerome who was adjusting her bed rails. He told her that she must have been dreaming because she had nearly fallen out of bed trying to reach for something that wasn't there.

Doctor Jerome may not have seen her mother, but Lila had no doubt in her mind that she had been there with her. Although she was still unable to put any weight on her leg, she was making some progress. By the end of day two, Lila was able to think more clearly and asked Doctor Jerome if he would check on Patty Miller for her. He didn't know much about Patty except what he read in the papers at the time she was found. Lila explained how she was doing the last time she saw her and he made a promise to visit her later that evening.

Nurse Margaret came by twice that day insisting she was only there to check on her patient, Lila Fern. Hoping to shed some light on Nurse Fiona's absence the doctor asked Margaret if she knew why she had missed her shift that day. This was the first time he experienced how truly nasty she could be. Nurse Margaret smirked, then said, "That useless tart couldn't tell the difference between a bedpan and a mop. I'm glad she's gone, now maybe I can get back some order around here."

Doctor Jerome replied, "Are you saying she left and isn't coming back?"

Nurse Margaret laughed as she told him, "She was always interfering in my work so I got her fired and if I had known it was that easy, I would have done it a long time ago."

Again, Lila had heard what she was saying. The news was disturbing as she realized that both Patty and April relied on Nurse Fiona for so many things. If not for her, they would never receive the care they needed and would end up rotting in their dirty bed linens. Now Lila couldn't be sure that either one of them was safe.

~

By day three, Lila had begun to regain her strength and she realized the fifteenth of August had come and gone. The night nurse, Alice Craw, had been with her most of the night and Lila was thankful for that, but now she was desperate to hear how Patty was. Doctor Jerome had promised to look in on her before leaving the night before and said he would come by first thing to give her an update. She also had another favour to ask, she needed him to pass a message on to Loraine to see when Patty could be moved out of Hillside and to let her know about her accident.

Lila could see by the look on Doctor Jerome's face that the news wasn't good. He told Lila that when he went into her room, Patty wasn't there. "According to one of the cleaners, Patty hadn't been responding at all yesterday and Doctor Asher became concerned. He later returned with Nurse Margaret and two orderlies who took Patty out on a gurney. She also said that when she asked Nurse Margaret how she was doing that evening, she had said to her that it was none of her business."

Doctor Jerome had been late that morning as he had attempted to find out where they had taken Patty, but he could not locate Nurse Margaret or Doctor Asher. He did say that he had left a message for the doctor and hoped to hear from him shortly.

Lila knew that this news was not good. If Patty was not responding, shouldn't she have been brought to the infirmary or sent to the hospital? Doctor Jerome agreed with her, but he didn't want to jump to any conclusions and preferred to wait until he spoke to Doctor Asher directly.

It was agony not knowing what was going on and despite Lila's often excruciating pain, she continued to refuse her medications. Hoping to keep a clear head, she would suffer in silence all morning but by noon, Lila couldn't stand it any longer and begrudgingly accepted her medication. Within the hour, she was pain-free and fast asleep.

That afternoon as Lila slept, Ernest had his lawyer look over the contract that Loraine had signed. Unfortunately, she did sign and initial where it mentioned that visitors were not permitted into the infirmary. Charles Renfrew did have one suggestion, but before he mentioned it, he asked Loraine, "What is your greatest concern?"

Loraine responded, "Lila's well-being, of course."

He then turned to Ernest and said, "Call Doctor Albert Lloyd, there is nothing in this contract that excludes her primary physician from visiting her, if he feels the need to." Ernest thought that was a brilliant idea, if they couldn't see Lila in person, the doctor could report back with her progress. Knowing this could take a few days to sort out, Charles said, "In the meantime I can ready the documents to have her transferred to Stanford Creek Sanatorium, along with Patty Miller." April Sampson, wasn't mentioned at this time as Lila had not been able to convey her message about this young girl's plight to Loraine.

It was almost three in the afternoon before Lila's medication wore off and she began to come around and the minute she opened her eyes, she asked about Patty. Worryingly, Doctor

Jerome hadn't heard from Doctor Asher or Nurse Margaret that day even though he knew that they were both in the building. Lila had experienced several bad dreams that morning, one of which had her attending Patty's funeral. It was horrible not knowing what had happened to her, and she asked Doctor Jerome again if he could go back to her room to see if she was there. He could see how upset she was and immediately left the infirmary to have another look in Patty's room. He also wanted to know what had happened to her, something about this whole situation was very disturbing.

Lila closed her eyes and although she didn't want to, she drifted back to sleep and found herself in the same dream that she had had earlier. As she stood over Patty's grave and dropped a rose onto her coffin, she suddenly heard her say, "Please, Miss, can you tell me why I am here?" Lila tearfully replied, "I'm so sorry, Patty, I tried to save you."

Just as the words left her lips, she awoke to see Nurse Margaret standing over her. Disregarding the doctor's orders to keep her leg elevated, she sat straight up, looked in her eyes and said, "What the hell have you done to Patty?"

Nurse Margaret smiled as she moved in a little closer, then she whispered in Lila's ear, "Oh, don't worry, Lila, you will see her soon enough. And by the way, did I mention that April Sampson's mother died yesterday? The poor girl has no one now. Isn't that a shame"?"

This only infuriated her more and Lila used every bit of strength she had inside her and pushed Nurse Margaret so hard that she fell into the dressing table, knocking the supplies to the ground. Just as she got up to retaliate, Doctor Jerome came into the room. He could see that something had happened and as he stood in the doorway he turned to Lila and said, "Are you all right, did she hurt you?"

Nurse Margaret then shoved the doctor aside and left the

infirmary without saying another word.

Doctor Asher hadn't been as helpful as Lila thought he would be. All he had to say was that Patty was failing and that he had transferred her to Orillia's Memorial Hospital. Lila was sure he was lying as Nurse Margaret had already suggested to her that Patty was dead. Doctor Jerome had already put in a call to the hospital and was awaiting a response. Now all Lila could do was wait.

Back in Elmvale, Loraine anxiously anticipated Doctor Lloyd's arrival. He had been delayed and was expected to come into town early the following morning. Ernest's lawyer had already filed the paperwork to have Patty Miller moved to Stafford Creek Sanitorium. Everything was in order and if all went well, Lila would also be transferred there temporarily and then be home by the end of the week.

This whole process seemed so long to Loraine, but she had forgotten that in order to have Andrew Potter believe that everything was above board, they had to continue the ruse. This way they could get the information needed to expose Hillside's atrocities. At this point, no one wanted Mr. Potter to know that Lila had been admitted solely to gather information. They also didn't want to set off any alarm bells just in case he attempted to cover up his involvement. Ernest's lawyer said that he was confident that they would have enough to shut him down, but he warned them that they still needed concrete evidence. This included the three dead bodies that still remained in the wooded area behind Hillside.

At this point, all Loraine wanted was to know that Lila was safe and until then she couldn't rest. To make matters worse, Isaac was in town and had come by demanding information about his wife. Ernest had to step in when he began insulting Loraine and, as expected, blaming her for Lila's decision to go to Hillside in the first place.

It took a while before he would listen to reason and by the end of his visit, he did what was right and apologized to Loraine. Deep down, Isaac knew that no one could have changed Lila's mind. She was as painfully stubborn as her mother when she made her mind up. Isaac left that afternoon knowing that his wife would soon be home, but he still felt very uneasy about what he had learned during his time with Loraine and Ernest.

As promised, the next morning Doctor Albert Lloyd arrived on the first train into Elmvale and for the first time in days, Loraine was feeling much more confident. Loraine explained to the doctor everything that she had learned so far and how she had come across the unmarked graves on the Hillside property. He was shocked to hear about the condition of the dead body and had a litany of questions he wanted answers to regarding the burial of the two unnamed infants. How did they die, why were they placed behind the asylum and who had given birth to them? Without examining the bodies, he could not make a conclusive diagnosis as to why any of them died, but he was determined to find out. He did tell Ernest that experimenting on a corpse was a common practice, but if the person had been alive when it occurred, Hillside would have to be held responsible for the death.

On the way to Hillside, Loraine began fretting again about what condition they would find Lila in. To add to her anxiety, once they arrived at Hillside they were immediately met with resistance. Two unknown attendants stopped them from entering and told them that Mr. Potter was far too busy to speak to them that day. Charles arrived just as they were being refused entry. He was armed with a letter demanding Doctor Lloyd be given immediate access to his patient, Lila Fern. He then insisted he hand the letter to Mr. Potter personally. Since the attendants were threatened with legal consequences, they stood away and allowed him to enter.

Loraine, Doctor Lloyd and Ernest, along with Charles entered Hillside, only to find more resistance from Mr. Potter. A shouting match soon began between Ernest and the owner. Charles then intervened and asked that he speak to Mr. Potter alone. Ernest reluctantly agreed and a few minutes later, Charles came out of the office smiling, and an attendant appeared and asked Doctor Lloyd to follow him to the infirmary. Whatever Charles had said had worked, and Loraine couldn't wait to hear how her friend was doing.

Doctor Jerome hadn't been informed of any visitors and at first questioned Doctor Lloyd about why he was there. Once he understood, he directed him to Lila. Doctor Jerome then allowed the two to talk privately as he attended his other patients. Their visit lasted over an hour as Doctor Lloyd examined Lila's fracture and was pleased with the care she was finally receiving.

Lila spent the rest of the visit explaining what she had discovered at Hillside. Although he had heard about some very questionable asylums, this one was among the worst. There wasn't any doubt in his mind that this place held some horrific secrets and needed to be closed down for good. He also wanted to know more about Nurse Margaret. She seemed to be an instigator in much of what happened here and he needed to know why a woman of her status had so much say. Something very disturbing was going on there, and he hoped that Ernest's private investigator would uncover the truth. He was also still very concerned about how two infants ended up buried behind this property.

Just before the doctor left the infirmary, he told Lila that he would have her moved out of Hillside the following day. She had requested going back to Elise's to recuperate and he felt that this was a splendid idea. Her weight loss was very noticeable and it was best in his mind that she went there instead of another institution, this way she could get some proper nutrition and spend time with her family. This was such a relief as Lila missed Isabel terribly, and she still held on to some concern that Nurse Margaret may follow through with some of her threats. She knew that if it wasn't for Nurse Fiona and Doctor Jerome that she might have ended up in the cellar on top of a cold steel gurney.

Just before Doctor Lloyd was leaving the infirmary, Lila asked if he could do her one other favour. "Doctor, I know you are a very busy man, but can you please have a quick look at one other patient today. Her name is April Sampson and the last time I saw her she was very poorly and beginning to lose the will to live."

She also explained her concern for her safety since she had no family ties and how she had been terribly worried that April might be Doctor Asher and Nurse Margaret's next victim.

Doctor Lloyd was happy to speak to her and asked Doctor Jerome to accompany him in case one of the orderlies tried to stop him from going there. Some of the men that worked there seemed more like thugs to him and Doctor Lloyd was far too old to deal with any further confrontations.

Twenty minutes later, Doctor Lloyd came rushing down the stairs and without speaking to Ernest or Charles, he barged into Mr. Potter's office and demanded he call an ambulance immediately. Loraine initially thought this was for Lila and started screaming. It wasn't until Doctor Lloyd explained that the ambulance was for April Sampson that Loraine finally calmed down.

14

As Loraine waited for Doctor Lloyd to give her an update on Lila, she watched to see two ambulance attendants rushing past her. The look on the doctor's face was very telling, concern and disbelief was written all over it. Within minutes the attendants were bringing April out on a stretcher and all Loraine could see was that her head had been shaved as if to prepare her for surgery. Her face seemed so small, almost child-like, and although her eyes were open, they were sunken back in her head. Loraine would later tell Ernest that she thought there was no life left in her eyes.

Within ten minutes of calling the ambulance, April was on her way to Orillia's Memorial Hospital. Doctor Lloyd didn't have the heart to tell Lila and decided to leave this dreadful news up to Loraine. Once April was on her way, he came back inside and gave Loraine, Ernest and Charlie a proper update on Lila's condition.

To their relief they discovered she was alert and recovering well from a fractured leg and would be leaving Hillside the following day. Doctor Lloyd would speak to Andrew Potter to let him know and to also inform him of April Sampson's condition.

Although her condition was grave, he held out some hope that she would survive. He told Ernest privately that without his intervention, April would probably have died later that same day.

Loraine asked that Doctor Lloyd not expose anything about Lila or why she had come to Hillside in the first place. She knew that one of the orderlies that had been following her was dangerous and she didn't want him knowing anything until Lila was safe and back at home where she belonged. Doctor Lloyd promised that he would never disclose a word to anyone about this, but he did want to confront Mr. Potter about one of his nurses and the role she must have played in April Sampson's current condition.

As a man who took an oath to "Do no harm" he simply couldn't understand how a nurse could purposely torture and possibly kill the very patients she was hired to look after. At this time, no one knew the whole story behind Lila's fractured leg and how Nurse Margaret had deliberately left her on a dirty floor for two hours. This along with April, who was now fighting for her life, was enough to turn his stomach. Whoever Nurse Margaret was, she certainly wasn't a caregiver.

Once Loraine was satisfied that Lila was okay, she and Ernest headed back to Elmvale to give Isaac, Elise and Mavis the good news. Doctor Lloyd was still waiting to see Andrew Potter and afterwards he was going to head to the hospital to look in on April, before going to his hotel for the night. Charles was on his way back to Elmvale to speak to Ernest about representing his wife and Lila if it came to that. At this point he didn't know the extent of information that Lila had collected and he simply wanted to be prepared in case Mr. Potter decided to file a complaint against her and Loraine.

After waiting for almost an hour, Doctor Lloyd was finally called into Mr. Potter's office. By now he was so frustrated that the minute he saw him he screamed, "How the hell did you allow this to happen? This place is not for ill patients, or for the families believing they are getting proper care, it's a bloody brick building filled with inept individuals, where most of these unfortunate souls will end up dead long before their time and no one, not even you, Mr. Potter, will take an ounce of responsibility!"

Mr. Potter glanced at his watch, sat back in his chair, lit a cigar, then smugly said, "Are you finished?"

Doctor Lloyd wanted to wipe the smug look off his face, but he was a man of integrity and he did not want to sink to his level.

Once Doctor Lloyd was able to speak without shouting, he said to Mr. Potter, "No, I am not finished, now you tell me how a perfectly healthy teenager can enter this facility simply because her mother couldn't care for her daily needs and end up less than a month later on the verge of death?"

Mr. Potter smiled as if this was amusing and said, "I suppose she wasn't as healthy as her mother would have you believe."

All this did was make the doctor angrier and as he got up to leave, he said, "Tell me, Mr. Potter, do you have any idea who I might be talking about?" Doctor Lloyd could see him trying to figure out who this might be and as he opened the door, he stopped but didn't turn around and sarcastically said, "I thought as much."

This had been a very long day for the now seventy-year-old doctor, but he still felt the need to go to the hospital and see how April was doing. During his lengthy career he had only lost a handful of patients but each one that he couldn't save, had left its mark. Now with an overwhelming sense of doom lingering within him, he made his way up to the hospital.

～

The next morning as Doctor Jerome prepared Lila for her transfer, Nurse Margaret came into the infirmary to see if the rumours about her leaving were true. Lila felt much stronger and far more confident than she had in weeks and as the doctor gathered her belongings, she looked directly at Nurse Margaret and said, "This isn't over, not by any stretch of the imagination and you will pay dearly for what you have done, I will make sure of that."

Sadly, at this time, she did not know for sure if Patty was still alive, and she had no idea that April had been transferred to the hospital or that her condition had been downgraded from critical to grave.

Nurse Margaret just smiled at Lila, then left quietly without making a comment; she wasn't really bothered by her threats and, in fact, she still had no idea who she really was or why she had come to Hillside in the first place. All she knew was that a patient was being transferred into another facility and she didn't ask why.

Although Lila was anxious to leave, the morning of her transfer was bittersweet. She had come to know Gladys and Esther, and wondered where they would go once this place was shut down for good. Lila described them as being very sweet and compassionate women, who sadly became victims of their husband's authoritarian views and who should never have been admitted to Hillside in the first place.

Loraine, Ernest, Doctor Lloyd and Billy were all anxiously waiting in the lobby for the transfer to begin. Doctor Lloyd had been there early to make sure that Mr. Potter had signed the release and now he would accompany Lila to Elise's home before going back to the hospital to see April.

Loraine ran to Lila as the attendants wheeled her down the hallway. Both women held on to one another for several minutes and cried. The whole ordeal had taken its toll on both of them but Lila had paid the ultimate price. Her emotional well-being had been compromised as well as her physical health. Thin, weak and still recovering from a compound fracture that would never heal properly, Lila would now go home and face her husband who was still very angry that she had risked her own life, without any regard for him or their baby daughter.

As she and Loraine exchanged information on the way back to Elise's, a priest was standing over April Sampson giving her the last rites. Overnight her breathing had become very laboured, a sure sign that she was not long for this world. Unable to reach Doctor Lloyd, the decision to bring in a priest was made by consensus. No one, not even the specialist, felt that April would recover. At nine thirty that same morning, she took her last breath.

Lila's return was met with a barrage of questions as everyone was concerned about her current condition. Elise and Mavis fussed over her as Lila held Isabel in her arms. Unfortunately, Isaac wasn't so welcoming. He was so upset with what he called "her irrational behaviour" that he would return to London that same afternoon after spending less than two hours with his wife. Although unhappy that her husband seemed to be abandoning her, she understood his concerns but that didn't mean she would have changed anything. Without her knowledge and first-hand experience, places like Hillside would keep operating and remain the dumping grounds for anyone who simply wanted to be free of their responsibilities. Lila knew deep down that Isaac loved her and that he just needed some time to himself to come to terms with what she had done.

On the other hand, Elise and Mavis were thrilled to have her home, they smothered her with acts of kindness and insisted they look after her and Isabel until she was ready to return to London. Lila had missed Isabel so much she wouldn't put her down the entire day. Her stay in Hillside had given her time to think about what she really wanted in life. Unbeknown to Isaac or anyone else, she had no plans on ever returning to London. Now back home with people who loved and supported her, she knew in her heart that she should never have left in the first place. Lila also felt guilty for not being home when her mother needed her the most. Whether it was guilt from not being here when her mother became ill or something entirely different, Lila had made up her mind; Elmvale was where she belonged.

Under doctor's orders to stay off her feet, Lila managed to stay put for less than two days. Unable to get any further information on Patty Miller, she and Loraine decided it was time to visit Orillia's critical care unit to make sure she was there. Doctor Lloyd had already left Elmvale, as he had been called back to London on an urgent matter. Sadly, he had left in such a hurry that he had not been told that April Sampson had died. Her thin, cold body now lay on a stretcher in the morgue awaiting an autopsy. Unfortunately, Lila had it in her mind that April was still at Hillside awaiting her transfer to Stafford Creek when she finally arrived at the hospital.

Luckily, Ernest was friends with Doctor Shipman, Orillia's current administrator, and the women were allowed to move freely albeit slowly due to Lila's crutches around the hospital. Their first stop was the critical care unit where they came across several patients, none of which looked anything like Patty Miller. Lila was hoping that Doctor Asher hadn't lied about Patty being there, but after speaking to the nursing staff, she came to realize that he had been.

Just as they were about to leave the floor, a nurse came over to tell them about an admittance from Hillside that they had received less than two days earlier. She had no idea who the girl was, only that she had come into their facility in critical condition and had died the following day. Lila's thoughts went directly to Patty and she insisted she see this young girl before leaving the hospital. Loraine tried to be the voice of reason and told Lila, "Even if this is Patty, do you really want to remember her like this?" Lila knew that Loraine was right, but she just had to know.

Back in Elmvale, Billy had compiled a lot of damning evidence about Hillside, including having in his possession a number of photos just waiting to become front-page news. He knew that it wasn't time to run his articles as he had discussed this already with Loraine and Lila. They needed to go over everything together and then Loraine, Lila and Ernest, along with their lawyer would take this evidence to the police. They not only wanted to shut down Hillside for good, they wanted criminal charges brought against Andrew Potter, Margaret Reid and Doctor Asher. Lila was also considering a class action lawsuit on behalf of all the patients that suffered at the hands of these monsters. This would mean going through every patient's file that had come into contact with Margaret Reid and Doctor Asher during their time at Hillside. Billy was sure that they would find some damning evidence and eventually have enough to bring Andrew Potter to his knees. All he ever cared about was money and if this went according to plan, he would not only lose the income from Hillside, he would lose his other properties and possibly his own home.

As Billy continued to sort through the information he had already received from Loraine and Lila, Mr. Potter met with two other shareholders. They had heard rumours about a possible investigation into some criminal activity that had occurred at Hillside and they were considering pulling out their funding and reinvesting elsewhere. Andrew Potter assured the investors that this was the furthest thing from the truth and after several hours of discussions, he was able to convince them to continue investing in Hillside's future. Although he owned sixty per cent of the shares in Hillside, he knew that without their money he could not live the same lifestyle that he had become accustomed to. Spoiled after years of getting whatever he wanted, including extensive travel with numerous beautiful women at his side, he certainly wasn't ready to give that up and he would fight till the end to keep it.

Lila on the other hand was fighting for something that would eventually make a difference in the lives of the unfortunate patients still living in a place she called hell on earth. She did not care about money, or the status of having taken down one of the wealthiest men in Simcoe County. All she cared about was the people that were still being neglected and tortured inside Hillside Asylum by the very people that were there to care for them.

As Loraine and Lila entered the morgue that afternoon, an overwhelming scent of death hung in the air. Lila gathered the nerve to have a look under the sheet that covered the corpse. Loraine held Lila's hand as she slowly uncovered the body. She was expecting to see Patty Miller lying there, but when she revealed April Sampson's emaciated body, Lila became off-balance and if not for Loraine's help, she would have fallen onto the floor. A few seconds later she sat down beside April's bruised and battered body, covered her eyes and began sobbing inconsolably. Lila was so distraught that Loraine called a doctor in to see her.

It had all been such a shock. April Sampson had had such a promising future. She was kind, thoughtful and intelligent and now she was barely recognizable. Her head was completely shaved, her body looked like a skeleton and there were burn marks on her wrists and temples, and numerous stitches that stretched across her forehead.

Lila would have to be sedated and kept overnight in the hospital, leaving Loraine to go back to Elmvale and reluctantly let Elise and Mavis know why she wouldn't be coming home. This wouldn't be easy as Lila had told them she was simply going out for lunch that day, hoping to put their minds at ease since they were still worried about her recovery, and she was ignoring the doctor's orders to rest.

April Sampson's autopsy was also performed that evening and it revealed some other disturbing news. This very sick young girl had not only been experimented on, she had been raped and it had occurred just shortly before she came into the hospital. Whoever the man was who had forced himself on her, had done so when she was in a semi-conscious state and unable to call out or fight off her attacker. This despicable revelation would never be shared with Lila, as the coroner felt that she was far too delicate to hear it.

15

The very next morning, Lila was back at the morgue asking questions about April's untimely death. Doctor Philbin explained that she had died from an infection that had entered her brain and that this was likely caused from a contaminated instrument that must have been used at the time of her lobotomy. According to the doctor, he had found more than enough proof still imbedded into her skull that would prove his theory.

"This type of surgery is not unheard of in some of the asylums, but it is always done under strict guidelines and only on the most disturbed individuals."

Lila knew that April was not only sane, she was bright, compassionate and extremely kind. Her only disability was that she was unable to take care of her daily needs and she was placed at Hillside merely because her mother's health was failing and she could no longer care for her. Doctor Philbin concluded that her death was the direct responsibility of Doctor Asher's decision to do an unnecessary surgical procedure on a young girl who was already weakened by dehydration and starvation. He also noted that she had several bedsores that were also infected due to poor hygiene and neglect and this was certainly down to the nurse in charge, namely Margaret Reid.

Lila had heard enough and as Loraine took her home that morning, Lila tearfully asked, "Do you think that Nurse Margaret had specifically targeted April to get back at me?"

Loraine hadn't thought about that; sure it was possible, but she didn't have the heart to say and instead, she replied, "Oh, don't be silly, dear, you know that Doctor Asher and Nurse Margaret chose her because April's mother had passed away recently and she had no family ties and no visitors since arriving at Hillside. I promise you; we will get to the bottom of this and they will pay for what they have done."

Whatever reason they had, the guilt of not being able to help her would remain with Lila for the rest of her days.

Exhausted, emotionally drained, and still in some pain from her fractured leg, Lila would spend the next few days locked inside her room, refusing to eat or speak to anyone. It would take a series of dreams involving her mother before she would gather the strength to carry on. Lila was now ready to continue to do everything and anything she could to see that those responsible for April's death were brought to justice. She was also determined to find out what had really happened to Patty Miller.

The following day, Ernest, Loraine and Billy met Lila at the constabulary, each one armed with a mountain of evidence that would surely expose Hillside's atrocities. They had a lot to say and at first everyone started talking over one another, all eager to tell the officers what they knew about Hillside. Both Constable Blake and Detective Broad were shocked at the allegations and could hardly believe that any of this was true.

It wasn't until Billy showed them the photos of Lois Russel and the two unknown infants that they were convinced what they were saying actually happened. Detective Broad told them that they would start an investigation immediately and that no stone would be left unturned.

Lila also urged them to find out what happened to Patty Miller and to look into the death of Constantine Rice, the woman she had seen in the cellar.

Detective Broad advised them all that they should stay out of Hillside until the investigation was complete. They assured everyone that they would be bringing in Nurse Margaret Reid and Doctor Asher for questioning. Lila also mentioned that they should speak to Nurse Fiona, who suddenly left Hillside and hadn't returned.

In the meantime, Ernest would have his lawyer begin a class action lawsuit against Mr. Andrew Potter. The lawsuit would address the multiple cases of abuse, both physical and psychological. It would also list the deplorable living conditions which included an abundance of rodents, contaminated food, insufficient heat, filthy rooms and overall patient care. Charles would demand Hillside Asylum c/o Mr. Andrew Potter compensate any patients that were of reasonably sound mind and pay for any future care of those that would not be able to reside independently. Mr. Potter would also be held accountable for any wrongdoing committed by his staff. The lawyer would also recommend that Andrew Potter never be allowed to operate any other asylum or sanatorium. The monitory pay-out would depend on how many patients had to be relocated and what their level of care was.

Ernest was satisfied with the lawsuit and told Lila, "Andrew Potter will not know what hit him tomorrow morning and if everything goes our way, which I believe it will, he will have to sell every one of his properties and possibly his home in order to satisfy this lawsuit."

Although money would never bring April Sampson back, or undo the harm that was done against so many including Patty Miller, it was satisfying to know that Andrew Potter would lose everything and never, ever be allowed to do this again.

Everyone knew that it would be a huge undertaking to transfer every patient out of Hillside and that it could take several months before any of this was resolved. In the meantime, Lila could rest assured that both Nurse Margaret and Doctor Asher would be removed permanently from the facility.

They left the constabulary that day feeling like justice would be done. It was now up to Detective Broad and Constable Blake to finish what Lila had started. In time they would uncover an array of crimes that would have the townsfolk wondering how this could have ever happened in this peaceful, rural community.

Billy would write a scathing article exposing the truth about Hillside. Now that Lila had safely returned to her family and everything was set in motion, Ernest would leave Elmvale and get back to work in London. Loraine promised to remain in Elmvale for as long as Lila needed her. This was a great relief to Lila, who didn't want to admit that she was beginning to feel overwhelmed.

Like her mother had done when she was alive, Lila held all her fears and uncertainties close to her heart. She never wanted to be seen as being weak or out of control. The thought of calling Isaac did cross her mind, but Lila felt he had been unreasonable and unmoved by what she had wanted to do. Mavis and Elise also tried to encourage her to call Isaac, but his last words to her left a lasting impression and despite their best efforts, she refused. Isaac did try to resolve things by writing to Lila after he returned to London, but sadly, his letters remained unopened.

Lila was so preoccupied with Hillside Asylum and finding Patty that little else mattered to her, other than her precious daughter, Isabel. She was and would always remain, the light of Lila's life. She vowed that by the time her daughter became a young woman, that she along with the others in the suffragette movement would have their voices heard.

∼

Within two days of speaking to Detective Broad, Hillside Asylum was officially the site of an investigation. Constable Blake and Detective Broad, along with several other constables, entered with a search warrant as Andrew Potter stood by demanding to know what was going on. Fortunately, on this day he was unable to stop them. As the other constables did a thorough search of the property, Detective Broad and Constable Blake immediately went to the basement and the minute they arrived, they heard a young girl screaming, "Please let me out, I promise I won't do it again!"

Detective Broad forced the door open only to see a sight that left him speechless. A girl, no more than thirteen years old, was sitting on a dirty cement floor, naked and shivering, with a heavy chain wrapped around her wrists making it impossible for her to move. Constable Blake spotted a key dangling about three feet away and immediately released her arms. After covering the child in a sheet, he carried her upstairs and straight into Andrew Potter's office. Before he could say a word, Constable Blake shouted, "Do you see this child, Mr. Potter? Do you see the cuts on her arms that the heavy chain has caused? Now tell me, sir, is this what you call exceptional patient care?"

The constable then turned to the child and said, "Now, young lady, you tell Mr. Potter who put you in that awful place and why."

Afraid to be punished again, the little girl turned away and refused to speak. Constable Blake said one last thing before leaving his office, "I assure you I will get to the bottom of this and you, sir, will be held responsible!"

Just as they turned to go, the child whispered in the constable's ear, "Nurse Margaret took me there. She had warned me not to wet the bed again, but I couldn't help it." Mr. Potter overheard what she said, but he was not moved and in fact he insisted they leave his office immediately.

Constable Blake could see how frightened this girl was and asked one of his officers to take her to St. Mary's Shelter, a home for girls run strictly on donations by the church and one that would never turn anyone away. He then returned to Mr. Potter's office where he confronted him again about the condition of this child and when he refused to take any responsibility, he pushed him up against the wall and held him by the neck while he calmly read him his rights. Once in handcuffs, he was escorted out of the building by another officer and taken to the precinct where he would be held until further notice. In the meantime, Nurse Margaret was being questioned by Detective Broad, who could be heard screaming at her to tell him the truth. Doctor Asher had left the building and was arrested a short time later trying to flee the area. He was found with several hundred dollars and a train ticket to the city of York. He later denied all allegations of abusing Hillside residents and insisted Nurse Margaret was the one they should be talking to.

Lila and Loraine were shocked at how much evidence Detective Broad had already discovered at Hillside Asylum in such a short space of time. The deplorable conditions were enough to shut it down for good, but they had also discovered the remains of more bodies, including an adult male who hadn't yet been identified and may never be, because of decomposition.

The medical examiner was brought in and asked to do an autopsy on each corpse, including the two infants. In the interim, a recently repaired wall was being looked into, as a police dog had indicated that there might be another corpse behind it. In the meantime, Nurse Margaret was handcuffed and taken in for questioning, but never confessed to any wrongdoing.

They also located Nurse Fiona who instantly indicated that it was Nurse Margaret who would order the procedures with Doctor Asher's blessing. Andrew Potter vehemently denied knowing anything about the patient care and within an hour of his arrest, he was released with charges still pending and instructed not to return to Hillside under any circumstances. A temporary manager was sent in from another facility and Nurse Fiona was reinstated. Doctor Edward Sharp would eventually be hired as a temporary replacement as the investigation continued. After six hours of intense questioning, Doctor Asher reluctantly admitted to experimenting on corpses but refused to admit that he had ever experimented on the living. He also denied having anything to do with the bodies that were found in the woods surrounding the asylum.

He was charged with indignity to a corpse and held in the precinct jail. Nurse Margaret also refused to admit any wrongdoing, but Constable Blake held her in custody on cruelty to a minor, neglect of her duties and assault. He would later find several patients who would confirm much of what Lila had said about her.

∾

Over the next two days Constable Blake questioned each patient at Hillside. He was accompanied by the new psychiatrist, Doctor Sharp, as he felt uneasy about the task at hand. During this time, he questioned a blind woman named Pauline Appleby. Pauline had been a long-time resident of Hillside as she had entered the asylum when she was just fifteen years old. She was a lovely, soft-spoken woman who the psychiatrist would later say didn't belong at Hillside. She told the officer that her grandmother had put her there after accusing her of ungodly behaviour. Her records showed that according to Sybil Appleby, she had witnessed her granddaughter reading the Bible, but Pauline had been blind from birth. This devilish act was enough to commit her to the asylum for the rest of her life. In reality, Pauline had memorized the Bible verses after spending much of her childhood in church. Unfortunately, she couldn't convince her grandmother of this and had been a patient of Hillside for almost nine years.

During their questioning, she revealed one other disturbing detail. She told Constable Blake and the psychiatrist that she had been assaulted by a man the previous year. She said, "I thought I was being taken for a bath by Nurse Margaret when I suddenly felt her stop and heard her talking to a man who I think was an attendant, the next thing I recall is being turned around and lifted onto a bed. I could still hear them talking and laughing and then I heard her leaving the room. I thought she'd forgot something, but when I felt him on top of me, I knew what was going to happen." Pauline added, "I did report this to Nurse Margaret, but she said I had imagined the whole thing."

It was obvious that she couldn't describe what he looked like, but she did say that he was overweight and he smelled badly. She added, "When l felt the child inside my belly, l didn't tell a soul, but soon l could no longer hide it and that's when Doctor Asher moved me into the infirmary."

When Constable Blake asked, "What ever happened to that child?" Pauline replied, tearfully, "They told me he didn't live."

Later that same afternoon the name Constantine Rice came into a conversation the detective had with Alberta Clarke. According to Alberta, Constantine had been her roommate for over a year when suddenly she went missing and a new patient was assigned to her bed. Alberta clearly had several reasons for being inside Hillside and her mind was that of a child who had never grown up and, unlike Pauline, she was loud and abrasive at times.

During the questioning she startled both the psychiatrist and the constable by telling them that Constantine was already dead and her body was sold to British travellers who paid a great deal of money for it. When asked, "How do you know this, Alberta?" She'd replied, "Because the nurse told me when she gave me her blanket." She described the nurse as being very pretty but one that was usually mean to her. This sounded just like Nurse Margaret, as many of the other patients described her this way.

When Alberta was taken back to her room, Doctor Sharp told the constable, "There could be some truth to what she's saying, but you must understand, much of what she says could be just something she imagined."

Constable Blake later checked into Alberta's records and found out that she did share a room with Constantine Rice, who had been reported missing twenty-six days ago by Nurse Fiona. Not one staff member had reported her disappearance to the police and since she was a patient with no family ties and few assets, no one had bothered to look for her. To confirm Pauline's statement that she had given birth to a baby boy recently, Constable Blake spoke to Doctor Jerome and he confirmed everything she had said, except that the baby had been born a stillbirth.

"The infant was viable and taken into the care of the Holy Cross orphanage." Constable Blake then produced the photo of a male infant found buried in the woods behind Hillside. Doctor Jerome couldn't be sure but he believed it could be the infant son of Pauline Appleby.

Doctor Jerome was very surprised to hear the infant had died, adding, "The child was a good weight and wailed so loudly the minute he was born, that I truly felt he would thrive." He denied delivering any other infants during his stay at Hillside and did not recognize the second child found in the woods.

When asked, "Who collected Pauline's infant from the infirmary?" He replied, "Nurse Margaret."

Now without a doubt in his mind, Constable Blake knew that Nurse Margaret Reid was just as Lila had described: evil and extremely cunning. Margaret Reid would be held in her tiny cell, awaiting her date with the judge.

Sadly, just hours after leaving Hillside that afternoon, Constable Blake would hear some devastating news. Patty Miller's decomposing body was found hidden inside a closet that had been boarded up. She had been wrapped in a dirty sheet and placed inside this old storage closet. An autopsy would later confirm that she had still been alive when she was placed inside there. Patty's lungs were filled with dust from the lath and plaster walls that were crumbling around her.

The medical examiner also found petechial haemorrhaging in the whites of the infants' eyes, indicating that they had probably been born alive and were later smothered. The autopsy done on the other body confirmed it was that of Lois Russel and revealed she had also died from infection caused by the experimentation that Doctor Asher had conducted on her. Constable Blake was also told that some of her brain tissue had been removed after her death along with her spleen and liver. The adult male was far too decomposed to render any firm evidence of foul play, but the coroner did say his liver and heart were missing.

Only the male child of Pauline Appleby could be positively identified, no other confessions of childbirth were made and at this point, no one knew for sure who gave birth to the baby girl.

Once Constable Blake had spoken to all the patients at Hillside, he went over to Elise's home to speak to Lila about Patty Miller. He felt that it was best she heard this from him as the families of some of the patients at Hillside were beginning to speak to the newspaper reporters. It was more than likely that this would turn out to be front-page news very soon. Billy wasn't ready to write his article and wanted to gather more information, but after seeing the reporters chomping at the bit for headlines, he began to compile his evidence in preparation for a front-page report that would expose Andrew Potter and the Hillside staff. His article would include the photos of the three deceased and would shock the entire town. Most residents of Elmvale and the surrounding area had no idea what was going on behind closed doors at this asylum.

Although Lila was horrified to hear how Patty Miller had died, they all agreed that her life had ended when her baby son, Ian, had passed away and death was no doubt a blessing for this young girl.

16

When Margaret Reid was told of the additional charges, she laughed at Detective Broad and said, "You have no idea who I really am, detective, but soon all will be revealed." He wasn't sure what she meant, but she was getting on his nerves and he replied, "You, Miss Reid, are a cold-blooded murderer and you will be hanged for your crimes; I know exactly who you are."

He could still hear her laughing when he headed back to his office. In another cell, just down the hall, Doctor Asher could be heard arguing with Chris Miller. Chris's lawyer was now busy appealing his charge of bigamy. Doctor Asher did not know Chris or even his connection to Patty Miller, but after spending a few hours together, the doctor asked to be moved. He found Chris to be obnoxious and crude as Chris bragged about his numerous love affairs, even discussing his perverted sexual fantasies. He seemed proud of what he was being charged with, referring to his former wife as being disfigured after her accident and that she had become dull and boring.

Doctor Asher would later find out who Chris Miller really

was, the man who had left his wife and infant to die while he enjoyed himself with another woman. This disclosure may have been a fatal mistake for Chris. The doctor had nothing but time on his hands, the longer these two men were forced together in this tiny cell, the angrier he became. Doctor Asher was far from a saint, but he was deeply disturbed by the reports he had read when Patty Miller was admitted to Hillside. The day after he had learned of what Chris had done, a side of the doctor was revealed that no one saw coming. In the early morning hours of August 24, Doctor Robert Asher would beat Chris Miller to death. He then hanged himself with his own bed sheets. They were both found dead by the guard. Robert Asher left behind a long rambling confession, which included his love affair with Margaret Reid. In parts of his confession he stated, "I didn't know I was capable of such despicable acts until I met Margaret."

His lengthy confession would certainly seal Margaret Reid's fate and reveal some more disturbing details about Andrew Potter.

As news trickled out slowly from the *Elmvale Examiner*, they were busy printing three times the amount of papers they usually did. A special edition ran twice that week as the public was demanding to know all the gruesome details. When the *Examiner* printed the story of Constantine Rice's disappearance from Hillside, an elderly man came to see Billy. His name was Walter Rice, Constantine's estranged husband. He hadn't come by because he was upset over her death, he just wanted to know if he would be getting any money from the pending Hillside lawsuit. After hearing that he had placed his wife there because she couldn't produce a son and that he hadn't even visited her during her stay, Billy tossed him out of his office, slamming the door in his face. This was occurring time and again as people came forward that had not bothered with their loved ones for years asking for compensation. Thankfully, the lawyer had made it very clear that only those that were involved with the patients during their entire stay at Hillside would be compensated. The money was not a free ride, it was to reimburse the patients who could live on their own and help to relocate the others at a later date. Families that were taken in by Andrew Potter's misleading advertisement would also be included in the pay-out, but this would be based on several factors.

The news of Chris Miller and Robert Asher's death spread through the town like wildfire, but surprisingly, Margaret Reid wasn't at all bothered by the news. They had been lovers for some time, yet all she had to say was, "We all die sometime."

Now that they had a detailed confession from Robert Asher, it was time to see if Margaret Reid would confess to the role she played at Hillside. Constable Blake was tired of her games, she would taunt him with vague statements, but she still wouldn't admit to anything. During several hours of intense questioning, all she would confess to was the affair she'd had with Robert.

During this time, the constable showed Margaret some of the evidence Lila, Loraine and Billy had gathered, including the gruesome photos of the corpses. Margaret's reaction was so bizarre that the constable had to leave the room and take a break. As he showed her each of the photos taken behind Hillside, she began to laugh hysterically. This disturbing reaction coming from a woman who had taken care of the sick and infirm made the constable begin to wonder about her own sanity.

In the meantime, the lawsuit against Andrew Potter had been filed and as expected was being contested by his lawyers. Rumours of Mr. Potter's involvement in what folk were referring to as the Hillside atrocities, were spiralling about the town. His confident exterior was beginning to crumble and some of his friends and colleagues had turned their backs on him. Andrew Potter may never spend a day in jail for the role he played at Hillside, but Charles would make sure that he would suffer a terrible financial loss.

Back in the constabulary, Margaret Reid's true personality was becoming very apparent. After a minor altercation with her cellmate one evening, she tried to strangle her. Clara Kimble was brought in for stealing from the mercantile after the manager refused to serve her when she insulted his wife. Clara was known for being rude and demanding and very few of her neighbours liked her. When she was put into a cell with Margaret, she started a conversation that quickly turned into an argument. Margaret was known for her sharp tongue and like so many others, she took an instant disliking to Mrs. Kimble. The argument began when Margaret told Clara that she should wear a veil to hide her ugly face and escalated when she said, "I imagine that your father had to pay a rather large dowry to marry you off, surely there isn't a man alive that would take you to his bed?"

Clara became so angry that she shoved Margaret, causing her to fall against the bars. A few minutes later the guard heard Clara gasping for air and found Margaret had wrapped her hands around her neck and was trying to strangle her. The guard later said that Margaret was whistling the entire time, as if she was thoroughly enjoying what she was doing. Clara survived and after being seen by a doctor was told that no permanent damage had been done. Detective Broad then had all her charges dropped against her and she was released into her husband's care.

The officers at the constabulary were dumbfounded. They had never met anyone like Margaret as most women behind bars became compliant, following the rules and adhering to their routine. Margaret was not at all compliant and she didn't seem bothered when the detective informed her further charges would be laid against her for assaulting Clara Kimble.

The fact that she was a nurse made this even more despicable. She didn't fit her role as a caregiver at all, and she actually seemed to find pleasure in others' pain. On a hunch that something wasn't as it appeared to be, Detective Broad decided to find out just who Margaret Reid was, where she had come from and her family ties. Since being incarcerated no one except her lawyer had visited. Constable Blake had made an off-the-cuff comment about Margaret a few days after she was arrested. He had said, "Miss Reid is more suited to an asylum then some of the patients 1 met at Hillside." Now the detective began to believe he might be on to something.

As he began looking into her background, he asked that Andrew Potter be brought back in for questioning. He also contacted the temporary administrator at Hillside and asked that her applicant file be released to the precinct.

Since returning to Hillside, Nurse Fiona had taken charge and managed to close the Preston Wing and stop any further needless procedures. She became a strong advocate for her patients as she felt they were being treated badly simply because of the label they were given or their social status. Unlike Nurse Margaret, Fiona was liked by everyone and the patients trusted her.

Over a few short weeks, she was able to comprise a long list of complaints from the patients who had once feared repercussions from Nurse Margaret if they spoke up. These were then handed over to Detective Broad. Each of the complainants told the same stories of their time in the Preston Wing, the isolation room and the electrified bath. They also said that when she was angry at them for any reason that she would withhold food and water for days at a time. Nurse Fiona also discovered a litany of complaints dating back to the time she was hired. Each story was more disturbing than the first, and Detective Broad quickly passed the information over to the Crown prosecutor. Although he never had any doubt in his mind that she was guilty, he felt that nothing should be excluded from the trial.

He owed it to the patients at Hillside, so they would know that their dreadful experiences at the asylum would not go unnoticed. Doctor Edward Sharp also felt this would be cathartic and may help to aid in their recovery. During this time, some of the very ill patients were being transferred out of Hillside. Their lives were now in the hands of kind, empathetic individuals who took pride in the care that they gave. Over the next few months, the others would follow, but for now, Doctor Sharp, Doctor Jerome, Nurse Fiona and a skeleton staff of attendants, cooks and cleaners did their best to take care of the rest.

Later that day as requested, Andrew Potter reluctantly came into the precinct accompanied by his lawyer Jed Saunders. Mr. Potter was still very angry at what had happened, and he still denied any knowledge of wrongdoing on the part of his staff. All assets pertaining to Hillside Asylum had been frozen and he was currently selling his other holdings to pay for his legal fees. The humility of being disgraced was the least of his worries. Money and power meant everything to him and he was already feeling the stress as, little by little, the lawyers took their enormous fees.

Once he found out why Detective Broad asked him to come in, he sent his lawyer home stating, "They are vultures, all grasping at a piece of my gold."

Detective Broad wasn't interested in his problems and he got straight to the point. "How did Margaret Reid come into your employ?"

Mr. Potter replied, "Sometime in late 1905 l believe she answered an ad placed by Doctor Parsons, the chief psychiatrist at the time."

"But l understand that you were in charge of hiring all staff at Hillside."

"Yes, and I asked a number of pertinent questions before anyone was hired."

"So what sort of questions did you ask Nurse Margaret?"

"l asked about her experience, where she had worked and why she chose Hillside. She had brought a letter of recommendation from an asylum that had closed its doors in 1904, and it was very convincing."

"And you believed that it was not a forgery?" At this time, the detective had not received her applicant file and Mr. Potter said it would still be in there.

"l had no reason to doubt her credentials, she told me her father was a highly respected doctor who taught her every aspect of her medical training, and that she worked with him until he retired in 1902."

The detective wanted to get as much information as he could and asked, "What was her father's name and where does he live?"

"Everett Reid and I believe he still resides in Holland Landing."

"I'm surprised that you can recall so much about Margaret Reid, is there more to this story than you're telling me?"

Mr. Potter replied angrily, "I don't know what you are insinuating, but I can assure you that there is nothing more to tell!"

Detective Broad wasn't so sure and felt he had a special interest in Nurse Margaret. There had been numerous complaints filed about her behaviour, yet he had done nothing about it.

During their thirty-minute interview, Detective Broad took impeccable notes. He planned on confirming all the information that Mr. Potter had given him. Oddly enough, he had been extremely co-operative that day and the detective felt that he was hiding something. If he could prove that he wasn't aware of what Margaret Reid was capable of, it was possible he could walk away relatively unscathed and be able to rebuild his reputation. Still, anyone who worked at Hillside knew deep down that he must have been aware of what she was doing, but without concrete evidence, Andrew Potter would end up with a bruised ego and a substantial financial loss but no time in prison.

At this time, he wasn't very important to the investigation. It was Margaret Reid's role that the detective felt was a priority. Robert Asher had paid the ultimate price, now it was her turn to face up to what she had done.

Soon after their interview concluded, a file containing Margaret Reid's applicant information was dropped off by a clerk from Hillside. As stated by Mr. Potter, a letter of recommendation was inside the file. The asylum's name was Cannington Care Asylum located in Chester Village only fifteen miles from Hillside. The detective knew Chester Village well, his mother-in-law owned a parcel of land there, but he had never heard of Cannington Care Asylum. The letter also stated that Margaret had worked there from 1902 to 1904 and that she had an exemplary record. It was signed by Doctor Frederick Johnson and Head Nurse Martha Richards.

Now the detective finally had something to go on. Margaret had been refusing to tell him anything about her past, where she had lived or who her parents were. A trip to Chester Village was now in order to confirm the existence of Cannington Care

Asylum. He also noted that Margaret had indicated her home address was 6226 William Street, Elmvale, Ontario. This was only ten minutes from the constabulary, so the detective decided to go later that day and possibly speak to her neighbours to see if they could shed some insight into her bizarre behaviour. She also listed her next of kin as her father, Doctor Everett Reid, but no address for him was given. Prior to leaving that day, the detective had Margaret brought back into the interrogation room.

He wanted to see her reaction once he told her about what he had found in her file. Each time he had asked about her past since her arrest, she had just laughed and told him it was none of his business. Now the tables were turning. Just prior to entering the interrogation room, he watched to see her rocking back and forth and whistling a church hymn. When she was like this, she seemed almost normal, angelic in a weird sort of way. This would all change when he displayed her file and he moved it just far enough away that she couldn't reach it.

Margaret stopped whistling, looked him in the eyes and screamed, "Give that to me now. If you know what's good for you, you will hand it over, do you hear me?"

The detective just couldn't understand this abrupt reaction, but that didn't stop him from continuing his interview. He was very used to interviewing criminals much scarier than Margaret Reid, and he wasn't intimidated by her threats. Each time she tried to reach the file, the chains attached to her arms and legs stopped her. This enraged her more. Once she finally stopped screaming, the detective sat back, lit his pipe and continued the interview.

Margaret was now refusing to speak and although he questioned her about her previous employer and the letter of reference, the only vague reaction he got was when he mentioned her father, Doctor Everett Reid. She didn't respond verbally to any of his questions, but the look on her face when he mentioned his name was very telling. Would this be the man that could shed some light about his daughter's actions and possibly explain why she had gone from a caring nurse, as written in her reference letter, to a cold-blooded killer, without remorse or compassion for the patients she murdered and tortured at Hillside?

17

After a brief visit to Hillside to check on the progress of the investigation, the detective went directly to Chester Village to speak to Doctor Frederick Johnson and Martha Richards. Since they were the ones who gave her a glowing review, he needed to find out what had changed since leaving her previous employment.

The village of Chester was situated in a valley of rolling hills and dotted with rivers and creeks. As he rode through the little hamlet, he wondered how such a cruel, heartless woman could have ever been any part of this beautiful landscape. As he travelled through the town, he couldn't find the Cannington Care Asylum anywhere. Knowing if it existed it would have to be in the local directory along with the addresses of Doctor Johnson and Martha Richards, all of whom he expected to interview that afternoon. After a brief visit to the postal outlet, he discovered that the clerk had never heard of the Cannington Care Asylum or Frederick Johnson, and they were not found in the directory. The name Martha Richards was somewhat familiar to her, she just couldn't remember where she had heard that name before.

She told the detective, "If an asylum by any name was here, I would certainly know it."

Thankfully, during his visit to the postal outlet, the local pastor came by to pick up his mail and informed the officer that the Cannington Care Asylum was still in operation and located about nineteen miles north-east of Chester Village in the town of Clarkson Heights. After concluding that neither Frederick Johnson or Martha Richards lived in the area, Detective Broad returned to Elmvale to visit Margaret Reid's last known address and speak to her neighbours. The visit to Cannington Care Asylum would have to wait for another day.

William Street was located right in the middle of town, and it didn't take long before the detective realized that he had hit another dead end. The address that Margaret Reid had given to Andrew Potter didn't exist. Frustrated, but not ready to give up, he decided to make his last stop of the day in Holland Landing. This is where Doctor Everett Reid had lived four years earlier, but this trip would also turn out to be of no help to his investigation. It seemed that no one the detective spoke to in Holland Landing remembered this man.

One elderly gentleman, a retired doctor who had lived in Holland Landing all his life, stated, "If Doctor Everett ever lived here, I would surely have remembered him, this town is very small and everyone knows their neighbours."

Now feeling terribly frustrated, the detective would leave Holland Landing no further ahead than when he started his search for answers that morning.

Not all would be lost that day as Lila Fern had come forward to shed some light on the real reason that Andrew Potter hadn't dismissed Nurse Margaret Reid from his employ. Although both her and Loraine were told not to return to Hillside, they did go back. Nurse Fiona had contacted Lila to tell her that now Nurse Margaret was no longer there, the staff were talking openly about an affair between Mr. Potter and Margaret Reid. After the officers left for the day, Lila and Loraine found the proof of this sordid affair in his office.

Tucked in behind some patient files was a small ledger book. Inside the initials M.R. were written on several pages as payments were being made to the owner of a flat ironically situated on Amelia Avenue, just up the road from William Street.

Ernest contacted the owner on a ruse that he was interested in purchasing the building. He also enquired about the two flats and whether they were occupied. It seems that the payment on one stopped recently and had not been occupied since. The woman who had lived in the flat was known only as Maggy and the payments came from none other than Andrew Potter.

This information was crucial to Andrew Potter's case. Without any time to lose, Detective Broad quickly called the owner to arrange a time when he could come by and have a look around. Mr. Walsh assured the detective that none of the tenant's items had been thrown out.

The next morning, Lila and Loraine stood out front of 73 Amelia Avenue awaiting Detective Broad's arrival. Thankfully, Lila's leg had healed very well and she was now able to climb the sixteen stairs that led up to the flat. Although it was highly unusual to have a victim of Margaret Reid's enter a possible crime scene of the perpetrator, Lila had insisted. She had heard that Nurse Margaret had stolen several items from the patients at Hillside and she was armed with a list, hoping to return them to their rightful owners once the police were done with them. It wouldn't take long to see that along with Margaret Reid's other more heinous crimes, she was also a thief. Inside her bedroom closet they found several items belonging to the patients and staff. One item brought Lila to tears as she came across the nightdress that her mother had given her. Unfortunately, all items pertaining to any thefts at Hillside had to be tagged and remain in the precinct storage until the trial was over. In due time they would be returned to their rightful owners.

The entire flat was a mess with furniture, lamps, food and clothing strewn everywhere, however, one crucial piece of evidence did emerge. Inside an old tea canister they found several notes and letters from Andrew Potter. Some were very explicit as he requested certain sexual favours. These letters and notes were all dated, beginning just weeks after Margaret Reid was hired by Andrew Potter. The last one was dated just before her arrest. Love letters from Doctor Asher were also discovered, but these were not nearly as explicit as Andrew Potter's were.

This was damning evidence that pointed straight at Andrew Potter and his unwillingness to fire a nurse he knew was guilty of all the crimes she was being charged with. Detective Broad felt somewhat vindicated that morning as every effort to put the two of them together, other than a working relationship, had failed until now. With energy to burn, he headed directly to Clarkson Heights after completing his search at Margaret Reid's flat.

Detective Broad had not been able to find out anything substantial about Margaret Reid's life before Hillside and he was hoping a visit to the Cannington Care Asylum would answer those questions. He knew to truly understand a criminal like Margaret you had to delve into her past. During the short time he had spent with her, she had acted very strangely as she would sometimes openly flirt with him and once when he got too close, she put her hand on his leg. Her bizarre behaviour was repeated with Constable Blake who said she leaned over and purposely exposed her bosom to him during an interrogation. Her expression was always the same, cold and soulless, and most of the officers just avoided any contact with her. Hoping to uncover something, anything, from her past, the detective made his way to Clarkson Heights.

When Lila returned home later that afternoon, she was surprised to see that Isaac was there waiting for her. Mavis and Elise took the children out for a stroll, leaving the couple alone to talk. They loved having Lila at their home, but they truly felt that she belonged with her husband. Lila had not told anyone except Loraine that she planned on staying in Elmvale, and now it was time to reveal this to Isaac. Lila still felt the burn of Isaac's comments but she had come to terms with why he had said what he said. The time spent away from him had not changed her heart and when he took her into his arms, she knew that although her love had been shrouded by her experiences at Hillside, Isaac was and would always be the only man she would ever love.

The love that Isaac felt for Lila had never changed and before he let go of her, he begged her to return to London with him. Lila hesitated, but not for the reasons Isaac was thinking and when he didn't get the response he wanted, he became frustrated and his tone changed dramatically. To make matters worse, he said, "I knew when you didn't take my name you never truly belonged to me."

Lila explained that it was simply a choice she made at the time and had nothing to do with how much she loved him. Sadly, whenever they argued he brought that up as if she had purposely chosen her father's name to hurt him, but once he realized he had made things worse, he asked one last time, "Lila, please come home."

Over the next two hours, they talked about everything that really mattered in their lives. Each one explaining what they felt was interfering in their happiness. Lila told her husband that she was unhappy in London and had been homesick for quite some time. Isaac explained that his wife's involvement in the suffragette movement worried him, as he knew that sometimes she put herself into dangerous situations. Now that they were able to openly discuss their feelings, they both decided on a reasonable solution and the very next morning, Lila revealed some of their plans to Mavis and Elise.

Detective Broad finally arrived at his destination an hour later than expected. Somehow, he had become lost and disoriented during his travels to the Cannington Care Asylum which was located in the middle of nowhere. This rather dark and ominous brick building was surrounded by old growth forest on each side and it was not visible from the road. The detective had ridden past it twice before even noticing it was there.

As he stood staring up at the barred windows, just a few feet from the ten-foot fence, a rather large and imposing orderly suddenly appeared. He had come out to question why he was there and what his purpose was for visiting the asylum that day. Once Detective Broad explained his reasons, the orderly unlocked the imposing metal gate. He was then told to wait in the foyer while he announced his arrival to the administrator. Detective Broad could see several rooms that had heavy metal doors on them; it instantly reminded him of a maximum-security prison. It was also eerily quiet compared to the Hillside Asylum, with only the sound of the caretakers going about their business. The windows were much higher than normal and out of reach to the patients. Some of the rooms also had bars across the doors. It was strange looking up at the locked doors that lined the halls just above a short staircase in the centre of the large foyer.

After a short wait, Mr. Baines came out of his office and introduced himself as Cannington's administrator. He was large, jovial man, that reminded the detective of Billy Carter. He welcomed him into his office, insisting he have a cup of tea and some raisin tea biscuits that had just been delivered from the kitchen. Mr. Baines, it seemed, was the complete opposite of Andrew Potter, with a welcoming demeanour and pleasant smile.

The detective knew that his job wouldn't be easy, but Mr. Baines seemed to take it all in his stride. After a few pleasantries, Detective Broad got down to business and handed Mr. Baines the letter that Margaret Reid used to secure the job at Hillside.

He asked, "Do you recognize the names Margaret Reid, Doctor Frederick Johnson or Martha Richards?"

Suddenly the administrator's face went white as a sheet, and the look he gave him had told the detective that something was very wrong. Without saying another word, he looked into his filing cabinet and took out a thick file folder, placing it down in front of the detective. The moment he saw it, he noticed a name written in bold letters, it was Martha Richards. Mr. Baines then insisted that the detective read it, but warned him that what was inside was extremely disturbing.

Inside was a photo of Martha Richards that looked very much like Margaret Reid. As he scanned the notes one thing caught his eye immediately, it read: *Martha Richards was found dragging the body of Everett Reid into the woods on Concession 13 in the town of Clarkson.* As he read further, he found that Mr. Reid had been poisoned and was already in a state of decomposition when she was seen dumping his body.

Mr. Baines then told the detective, "They also found the bodies of her parents a few feet from where she dumped Mr. Reid's body. The coroner had stated that they had also been poisoned."

The more he read, the more sense things were making and now all the pieces of this bizarre puzzle were coming together.

Martha Richards was originally placed in custody awaiting sentencing for the murders of her parents and Everett Reid in Clarkson. A short time later her defence attorney noticed some rather odd behaviour and changed his plea from not guilty to not guilty by reason of insanity. It was he that recommended a psychiatric assessment. Over a span of a few weeks, three different psychiatrists examined her and all concluded that she was mentally unstable and not criminally responsible for her actions.

Mr. Baines continued, saying, "In the fall of 1902 Martha Richards was found to be criminally insane and placed at Cannington Care Asylum for the rest of her natural life. She was ill with the flu when she arrived and placed in the infirmary. Somehow she managed to raise herself up enough to escape through a tiny window and she hasn't been seen since."

Detective Broad then read about the search conducted shortly after she went missing, but she had disappeared without a trace.

Mr. Baines added, "The townsfolk were terrified she would kill again and began locking their doors at night. No one felt safe here."

The search was eventually called off when the body of a young woman that resembled Martha Richards was found in Trout Lake. Everyone assumed it was her and the case was closed. Now Mr. Baines would have to face the facts, Martha

Richards was still very much alive and she would likely end up back at his asylum.

Mr. Baines told the detective that according to the psychiatric reports, Martha Richards had been diagnosed with some sort of mental disturbance when she was just a teenager. Her parents thought she was possessed by the devil. The local priest, Father Andrew Thompson, had performed an exorcism and assured Martha's parents that the devil had left her body.

For a brief time, she remained relatively quiet, attending school and helping with the chores around her home. When she met Everett Reid, her psychosis came back to the surface. Everett was married and although he thought Martha was a beautiful young girl, he had no interest in pursuing her. Martha then became obsessed with having him. He was just doing some handyman chores around their farm but Martha wouldn't leave him alone. From early morning until he left at six, she would follow him around like a puppy dog. Her behaviour became such an embarrassment to her parents that they had to let him go. Martha became unhinged and within a week of his dismissal, she had murdered them. The police later learned that she kept their bodies in the cold cellar for an extended period before dumping them into a field just steps away from her home. A few weeks later they found Everett Reid's body. Everett's wife Anna stated that Martha had continued to pursue her husband even after he stopped working for her father and she had warned him against speaking to her.

The news was both shocking and disturbing. Detective Broad now understood why the person that he thought was Margaret Reid seemed to have no remorse or empathy for the people she had hurt. Unfortunately, he also knew that this would change everything. Martha Richards could no longer be held responsible for the insidious acts of torture and cruelty she had done during her time at Hillside Asylum. The Crown prosecutor would have no choice but to release her back into the Cannington Care Asylum for the Criminally Insane. This was far from ideal, as most people that knew about what she had done had wanted to see her hang.

Mr. Baines had been very helpful that day, but the detective had one last question. "Was Martha ever schooled in nursing?"

Mr. Baines replied, "As far as 1 know, she had no formal training and, frankly, 1 find it very disturbing to hear that she was hired at Hillside considering her documents were nothing but a forgery. Any professional medical personnel would have seen right through her soon after she began to work there."

18

By the time the detective got back to the precinct, he was extremely excited to share his news with Constable Blake. He had been right all along; Martha was a lunatic and certainly should never have been able to obtain work in a place with vulnerable people. Now, his only question was what would the Crown prosecutor do with this information. He also wondered if further charges would be made against Andrew Potter, considering that he had hired someone unfit to work at his establishment and that he had carried on having a rather crude affair with during her entire time at Hillside.

That same afternoon, Detective Broad asked Billy, Loraine and Lila to meet him at the station house. They had all been an integral part in finding Martha Richards and exposing Hillside Asylum's dirty little secrets. The news came as quite a shock to them all and they now insisted that Andrew Potter be held responsible for everything that Martha Richards had done during her time there. Lila pointed out that he could have fired her from this position at any time, yet he chose to keep her there in order to satisfy his sexual desires without having any regard for the suffering that went on inside Hillside. This was simply outrageous and should never have happened.

Thankfully, the detective agreed wholeheartedly and planned on taking his information straight to the prosecuting attorney that same day. With a promise to keep them all informed, they left not knowing what was going to happen to either Andrew Potter or Martha Richards.

As promised, Detective Broad immediately made an appointment to see the new prosecuting attorney, Reginald Green. Luckily, he was well versed on Hillside Asylum and seemed to be expecting the detective when he arrived. Reggie, as he preferred to be called, was very impressed with the detective's work in finding out everything he could about Martha Richards and her connection to Andrew Potter. Within less than two hours after their meeting a warrant was issued for Mr. Potter. He would now be charged with obstructing justice, aiding in criminal behaviour and withholding evidence. Mr. Potter was now looking at ten years in prison, and Reggie was absolutely certain that he would be found guilty. Martha's case was not as cut and dry; he was doubtful that she would be found guilty of first-degree murder and advised the detective that he would be seeking life inside the same facility that she had been placed in originally. Either way, both Andrew Potter and Martha Richards would be sufficiently punished for their crimes.

The next day Detective Broad met with Martha Richards to discuss his findings. This meeting would only confirm her original diagnosis as her behaviour went from bizarre to downright insane. The minute she found out that he knew her real name she began to scream obscenities at him, threatening to murder his wife in front of him and then chop up her body and feed it to his children. Her behaviour had been so unnerving that he placed her inside a rarely used cell in the basement. Listening to her describe what she would do to his beloved wife had made him feel sick to his stomach. For the first time since meeting Martha Richards, he found out how truly disturbed she was.

Andrew Potter was remanded in custody, awaiting his trial. This time his overpriced lawyers could not get him out on bail. A few days later he agreed to a plea deal in order to save himself from the embarrassment of a lengthy trial. He pled guilty to the lesser charge of obstructing justice. He then signed over his two residential properties and Hillside Asylum in order to have two years shaved off his time and put a stop to the class action lawsuit. This would leave him almost penniless, but he would still have his home to go to when he got out. If he continued to pay his lawyers, he knew he would end up with nothing. Despite everything that had come to light, he continued to deny knowing who Margaret Reid really was, but he did admit that her behaviour at times was very odd. Andrew Potter would receive eight years for the role he played and end up with very little when he was released from prison in the summer of 1915.

Unfortunately, the news about Martha's transfer was not as satisfying. Cannington Care Asylum was at capacity and for now, she would have to stay in her cell until a room became available. Reggie could not tell the detective how long that might be but did assure him that the minute a room became available he would arrange a transfer.

For the time being, Martha Richards remained in the precinct lock-up and spent most of her days screaming obscenities at the guards and threatening every one that came near her cell. A court appointed psychiatrist who had spent a great deal of time with her, told the detective that she was a very dangerous woman, a true psychopath with absolutely no ability to feel compassion or remorse. Martha would become increasingly violent during her final days at the precinct and she would not accept her fate. As the days grew closer to her transfer, she became more violent, even throwing her hot soup at a constable, causing second degree burns to one side of his face.

By mid-September Isaac had returned to Elmvale with the news that Lila had been waiting for. He had quit his job and was ready to continue his life in Elmvale alongside his wife and child. The last time he was in town, the two had discussed everything openly and both agreed that they were always happier during their time here. Lila also had some news; she was planning on continuing where her mother left off. Midwifery was more than a way to make money; it was a way of connecting with other women and she knew that her mother would be very proud of her. Amelia had always encouraged Lila to take up the calling, but she knew that her daughter would have to decide this for herself. Only then would she know that this was what she wanted and that Lila wasn't simply abiding by her mother's wishes.

With Isaac back in town and Lila on the mend, both physically and emotionally, Loraine felt that it was time she left Elmvale and returned to London to be with her husband. This day would be bittersweet as Loraine had not only helped Lila through the worst days of her life, she was also an integral part of the investigation into Hillside's atrocities. Had it not been for her, Lila knew things may have been much different. She loved Loraine and respected her thoughtfulness and integrity. Now, watching her best friend board the train, Lila felt as if a piece of her heart was leaving too.

Back at the station house, Detective Broad was feeling frustrated as the mountain of evidence he and his constables had collected against Martha would never be heard in a court of law. He also knew that there was nothing further he could do to punish her for her crimes. Although she was considered criminally insane, he really wasn't satisfied with her sentence. Sending her off to the asylum for the rest of her natural life didn't seem like punishment enough. Thankfully, she was now one week away from her transfer and everyone in the precinct couldn't wait to see the back of her. The detective could tell she despised the idea of going back there as this was the first time since her arrest that she had shown any fear. The detective found some comfort knowing she would never be released back into society and would endure the same feeling of isolation that the patients at Hillside had endured.

A plan was made ahead of time to ensure that Martha Richards didn't try to escape. In order to be absolutely certain that this wouldn't happen, a psychiatrist at Cannington ordered she be put in a straitjacket prior to her transfer. He also insisted that two orderlies accompany him during their travels back to Cannington. The arrangements had been made and Martha was informed that her transfer was near.

During her final few hours at the precinct, Martha shouted some very disturbing threats at the detective and his constables. One of them disturbed Detective Broad more than the others as somehow she had learned the names of his wife and his two daughters. Martha shouted over and over, "You better watch out for your pretty young wife, Sara, and little girls, Francis and Rebecca, cause one day they may go missing, and I promise you that they will suffer the most agonizing death unless you release me this minute!"

Although unsettled, Detective Broad never reacted to Martha's taunts. Her appointed psychiatrist told the detective it was just very typical behaviour coming from a psychopath with no regard for anyone else but herself. He reassured him that Martha Richards would never be allowed back into society and would remain at Cannington under careful watch until the day she died.

Lila was also told about the threats against her and although she wanted to confront the woman that had left her to die, she decided that Martha wasn't worth her time or energy. Instead, Lila spent her free time looking for a new home for her, Isabel and Isaac. She would always be in debt to Elise and Mavis, as without their support these past few months, she knew that she would never have been able to come to terms with her mother's death. Now she needed to move on and begin the next chapter of her life.

Martha Richards' transition into the Cannington Care Asylum didn't come without problems. Despite wearing a straitjacket, she also had to be heavily sedated. It would also take four constables to hold her down as the doctor injected the sedative. Prior to that, she screamed and spat at the constables and tried to bite one of the attendant's hands. Considering her small stature, Martha was incredibly strong. The moment her strait-jacket was removed, she grabbed a chair and smashed it over a nurse's head causing grievous injury.

Now considered to be one of the most criminally insane individuals ever to reside at this asylum, Martha was completely isolated from the outside world and all the patients. In a nine by nine padded room, without a single window, she spent her days only being allowed out to bathe. Once a week, two large male attendants would escort her and remain standing by in case she attempted to injure the female staff. Her food was slid through a small opening at the top of the door and the tray was returned through the same access point.

Martha continually threatened anyone within earshot, telling them what she planned on doing to them and their loved ones when she got out. As the days went by, her anger became more intense and the descriptiveness in her threats increased substantially. She told one orderly she was going to take his young sister and bury her alive, but most people paid little attention to her outbursts. Detective Broad and Constable Blake were very relieved to have her gone.

By the end of September, Hillside Asylum had less than half of its patients as most of them had been relocated to another asylum. Gladys and Esther along with nine others were deemed of sound mind and moved into their own flats and hopefully, in time, would be able to adjust to life outside of the asylum.

Plans to give the two infants found in the woods behind Hillside a proper burial was in the works too, along with having Patty Miller, her son, Ian, and April Sampson moved into consecrated ground. Although the atrocities at Hillside Asylum would never be forgotten, by early October a calm had returned to this little town. Billy, Lila and Loraine were also ready to put this behind them, they had done exactly what they had set out to do: expose Hillside and everyone involved.

Lila, Isabel and Isaac finally settled into their own flat that was just a five-minute walk to Elise's home and once word got out that Amelia's daughter was here to stay, Lila had numerous enquiries regarding her services.

As Christmas approached that year, Billy was busy making final arrangements to distribute the toys he had collected, and Lila had just learned that she was expecting her second child. Everything was as it should be as the Elmvale residents prepared for the long winter ahead.

Hillside Asylum was now officially closed and although the body of Constantine Rice had never been found, the excavation of the woods behind Hillside had come to an end.

It wasn't until December 19 that Martha Richards would once again become a topic of discussion. Detective Broad was just about to leave for a long-awaited vacation with his wife and daughters when he got an unexpected visit from Mr. Baines who had some rather disturbing news about Martha Richards.

It seemed that his most notorious patient was now with child. The doctor had estimated that she would give birth somewhere between the end of February and the beginning of March. The physician that examined her also found that she had already bore a child and he believed that this would have occurred within the past year. Although she was questioned as to the whereabouts of this infant, all Martha would do when asked was break into hysterical laughter. No one knew for sure if the infant had been viable and they weren't about to get a straight answer from Martha.

The only good news Mr. Baines had was that since finding out she was with child, her violent outbursts had decreased. Detective Broad didn't believe for a moment Martha Richards could ever change, and he replied angrily, "I do not trust this woman and if I'm right the unknown female infant that was buried in the shallow grave behind Hillside may have belonged to her. The coroner stated that both of the infants found on Hillside property had been born alive, their lungs had expanded meaning they had taken their first breath. The female infant's body had decomposed more than the males and it was likely that this was the one that Martha Richards had delivered."

Mr. Baines agreed with Detective Broad and although her outbursts had subsided, he knew she was beyond help. If there was one thing he had learned working at the Cannington Care Asylum, it was never to trust anyone diagnosed as being criminally insane.

Before leaving that afternoon, he told the detective, "If the infant is viable it will go directly to the orphanage and far away from its mother. At least this way it will have a chance to live a normal life and hopefully it will eventually be adopted by a loving family."

For now, the detective decided not to say a word and although gossip still swirled around about what happened at Hillside, most people didn't dwell on it any longer. The case against Martha Richards was closed.

19

On January 3, 1908, the weather had changed dramatically as a massive snowstorm struck the region. Up until then there had only been a light dusting, which usually dissipated with the afternoon sun. Lila had been up all night trying to deliver a baby that had decided to wait until the wee hours of the morning to make his debut. After a very long night and a successful delivery, Lila went home to sleep after checking in on Isabel who was cuddled up beside her father.

A few hours later she was awakened by Jeremiah Johnson. His baby wasn't due for another six weeks, but Jeremiah insisted it was on its way. After dropping Isabel with Mavis, Lila quickly headed straight to the Johnson's farm. As she prepared Mrs. Johnson for delivery, she worried that the infant was going be too small to survive. Lila's mother had successfully delivered several tiny infants before and always said, "These special babies have a will to survive. As long as they are loved, they will thrive."

Lila kept saying these words in her mind as Mrs. Johnson screamed out in pain. Fearing the infant may have some difficulty breathing, she withheld any pain medication as it would sometimes slow the infant's heart rate.

After several hours of excruciating labour, Johnathan Carl Johnson was born weighing four pounds two ounces. Perfect in every way and after giving the mom strict instructions about keeping him warm, Lila left feeling confident he would survive. Elise and Mavis offered to keep Isabel that afternoon, allowing Lila to go home and rest. After a long hot bath, she got into her bed and fell fast asleep.

Less than an hour later she heard someone knocking at her door. Now feeling somewhat agitated because of lack of sleep, she opened the door to see someone she hadn't seen in ages standing before her. Nelly Harthstone, the current owner of the Miller property, had come by to bring her something that she knew would put a smile on her face. Nelly had been cleaning out the attic when she came across Amelia's old medical kit. As Lila gazed inside this treasure trove of bits and pieces her mother had collected over the years, she came across all her birthing tools including a set of forceps that Lila knew would have cost a month's wages. Seeing the forceps brought a tear to Lila's eyes as she knew that this tool would have been instrumental in delivering Ian Miller. Lila had thought that these had been lost forever, and she would be forever grateful to Nelly for bringing them home where they belonged.

Just before putting them all back into the beautifully crafted tin box, Lila found another surprise. Inside a sealed envelope marked with the initials EB, she found a beautiful photo of Elise with baby Charity. Few photos of this child had ever been taken and Lila knew it was irreplaceable. Sadly, Charity's death had been the beginning of her mother Amelia's demise, as she had blamed herself for her untimely death, just as Lila had blamed herself for Patty's death. This discovery brought back so many memories; some good but some she wished had never happened.

Despite feeling completely exhausted, Lila decided to head

into town to purchase a lovely frame for the photo she'd discovered. Elise had helped her through some very difficult days and giving her this photo was Lila's way of thanking her for all that she had done.

The snow that had blanketed the landscape reminded Lila of a portrait she had seen in London. It was as if the painter had sat in the middle of the town and captured it in all its glory. The white crystals that lay on the farmers' fields glistened in the sunlight and at least for that moment in time, Lila felt a sense of peace come over her that she hadn't felt in months.

Elise had no recollection of the picture Lila had so thoughtfully framed ever existing. Now, as she stared up at the photo that adorned the centre of her mantel, she couldn't help but mourn for the loss of her precious little girl and the friend that had saved her from her husband's brutality. This photo meant more to her than Lila would ever understand, and Elise was so very thankful that she had given it to her.

It had been an emotional day for all and after leaving Elise's home, Lila dropped Isabel off with her father to spend a few quiet moments at the cemetery with her mother. As she approached her grave that afternoon, she noticed a large bouquet of white roses laying in front of the headstone. After brushing the snow away from both her mother's grave and Ian's, she found another little surprise; a small wooden horse pulling a carriage lay on top of Ian Miller's grave.

Lila realized immediately that the toy was from Billy and she assumed the flowers were too. Billy Carter had the gentlest spirit and the kindest heart, and she knew that when he delivered the toys he collected throughout the year that no child would be forgotten. This wonderful gesture had reinforced what Lila had already known and she knew that wherever life took her, she would always be a better person for having known Billy Carter.

Sadly, the sense of peace and tranquillity that had arrived

with the first winter snowfall would suddenly be shattered by the news that Martha Richards had given birth to a son.

On January 19 and almost two months earlier than expected, Martha Richards was rushed to the infirmary shortly after her water broke. Her nurse, Jasmine Albright, had noticed that she also expelled a great deal of blood and was afraid she would bleed to death if not seen by a doctor. Within moments of her arrival, Doctor Peter Shield noted that the placenta had come ahead of the baby and he immediately began using pressure to remove the infant. Martha screamed out in pain and called the doctor several colourful names until she was given a small dose of opium. When this didn't seem to work, he gave her a little more. Doctor Shield then carefully expelled the placenta along with the infant, which was not breathing initially. To everyone's surprise the tiny boy who the doctor felt would die, began showing signs of life. Colour eventually returned to his face and lips, and soon he was breathing on his own. After the delivery, Martha was given another dose of opium as Doctor Shield removed the rest of the placenta. By this time, she was completely unaware of what was happening as the infant was taken to another room to be monitored, before being transferred to the orphanage.

For almost two days, Martha remained in a state between consciousness and sleep. The doctor surmised that the excessive blood loss along with the opium had contributed to her state. Martha's deep sleep was a blessing to the staff who often heard her screaming during the day and night. It was a relief not having Martha's loud, obnoxious voice reverberating throughout the asylum. By January 21 her four-pound three-ounce baby boy was well enough to be transferred out of the asylum and into the orphanage where he would later be adopted by a childless couple in Green Hill Township. The records were sealed to protect the adopted parents as well as the infant. Little was known about the adoptees except they were good Christians and caring individuals who longed for a baby of their own.

Back in Elmvale no one knew about the birth of this child except Detective Broad, Billy and Lila. There was no announcement and Martha Richards would never know who had adopted her son – most believed she didn't care enough to even bother asking. The baby's fate away from his biological mother was much more promising than it would have been if Martha had birthed the child elsewhere. Speculation from some renowned psychiatrists wondered if she had passed on her mental disease to her infant son. Some had begun studies of families who had members with either severe criminal behaviour or a diagnosis of being psychotic, and found that it was highly likely to affect an offspring if one or more parents were afflicted with this strange phenomenon. Now in its early development, it was neither proven nor disproven and was often dismissed as being unlikely to happen by several other psychiatrists. For now, Martha's child would be loved and cared for and Doctor Shield believed that nurturing the baby would help mould him into a fine young man. He for one did not believe that his mother's psychotic criminal behaviour would be passed on to him.

After the delivery, Martha didn't ask about the child nor did she concern herself with where he was taken. No one was surprised by her inability to have any maternal feelings. Martha wasn't capable of caring for anyone but herself. Every psychiatrist concluded that she would be a danger to others and should never be released into society. Her prognosis was not wrong, as Martha had the most deviant mind the doctors had ever come across.

For now, she would remain in the infirmary as the bleeding continued and she was sleeping up to fifteen hours a day. It seemed that nothing the doctor did had helped her and she wasn't showing any signs of responding to treatment. She had taken in a small amount of nourishment over the past few days, but her constant sleeping worried him. He was so concerned for her well-being that he eventually ordered her legs and arms to be untied. This was to avoid any further injury as she had tried to turn over many times and the leather straps had caused deep cuts to her ankles and wrists. Doctor Shield felt that she was far too weak to be of any concern and once the straps were removed, as expected, she turned on her side and went back to sleep. Disturbingly, this was her doctor's first fatal mistake. He had no idea just how vulnerable he had become the moment he released the straps.

It was now day five since she had given birth and still in the doctor's mind, her condition remained guarded. He was concerned at the amount of time she slept and he worried that there was a possibility that she could be bleeding internally. Doctor Shield had no idea she was faking the entire time.

Martha was a master of manipulation and each time a doctor or nurse entered the room, she lay perfectly still and pretended she was sleeping. Now that her arms and legs were free, she waited for the perfect opportunity to make her escape. Martha had watched and seen that there were times during the day when the doctor would leave the infirmary for approximately fifteen minutes. The spare keys to the front entrance and hallways sat in a locked case, just a few feet from her bed. She noticed that neither the doctor nor the nurses ever used those keys but they looked identical to the ones they carried. Now whenever the doctor left the room, she got out of bed and began to steal various items from the infirmary, tucking them under her pillow and out of sight. A surgical knife, two syringes and a container of opium were neatly tucked between the pillow and the pillow cover. Martha was very careful and by the time the doctor would return, she had already gotten back into bed, pretending to be fast asleep.

By day six, Martha had figured out exactly when the nurses began their shift change and she knew that at this point she had at least ten minutes before anyone would return to the infirmary. As she hid her hands under the bedding, Martha carefully withdrew a large amount of opium from the container, filling one of her syringes to capacity. Martha then turned to face the doctor's desk as he sat with his back to her, quietly doing his paperwork.

Methodically and without making a sound, she snuck up behind him and before he knew what was happening, she stabbed him in the neck with the opium filled syringe. This immediately rendered him helpless, and within a few seconds he fell unconscious. Martha then wrapped her arm with a towel and smashed the glass of the cabinet containing the spare keys. Once in hand, she ran toward the door which led to the main entrance. Only one orderly sat at the entrance, but he had not yet noticed her in the foyer.

Martha hid behind a heavy cabinet and when he left to check on something upstairs, she quickly tried to open the main door. She stood there trying one key after another until finally it opened, sounding an alarm that could be heard throughout the building. All available staff came running downstairs as the doors slammed behind her. It took only a few minutes to realize that Martha Richards had escaped once again. After concluding that Doctor Shield had not survived, every available staff member began searching the grounds and surrounding buildings. Minutes later, one of the staff returned to the building and called the police. Martha, who had been treated kindly by this doctor, had injected him with enough opium to kill a horse. Every one believed that she must have known that the amount she injected into his neck would be fatal. Determined to escape the asylum, like she had threatened to do so many times before, no one was surprised she would go to such great lengths, regardless of who got hurt in the process.

Detective Broad wasn't told about the escape until the following day. He had been out of town over the weekend and only found out by chance when he came across a roadblock on his way back home. After dropping off his family, he joined the massive search for Martha Richards. Once he found out how this had happened, he went directly to the Cannington Care Asylum to speak to Mr. Baines. By this time, he was so angry he could hardly contain himself.

He had been promised over and over again that Martha would never find her way out of his asylum. After announcing himself to the clerk he didn't wait to be escorted into Mr. Baines' office and burst through his door, instantly condemning his staff for being so careless. Once he was finished ranting, Mr. Baines tried to explain what had happened, but the detective wouldn't listen. It was only after hearing about the death of the doctor, who was set to retire that year, that Detective Broad calmed down. Mr. Baines, still visibly shaken, had only just returned from breaking the horrible news to the doctor's wife.

It wasn't long before the news of her escape began to spread throughout the town and when Detective Broad got back to his office, Lila and Billy were waiting for him. The news was devastating and Lila, Billy and the detective were fearing some sort of retaliation. Martha had threatened so many people that no one was taking any chances. Billy suggested putting a photo of her on the front page of his newspaper so everyone could recognise her and report any sightings. Detective Broad thought this was a great idea and went into the evidence drawer and took out one of the photos he had found in Andrew Potter's office.

In the meantime, the detective planned to move his wife and children into his mother-in-law's home just fifteen miles north of the town. Lila was told to warn Elise and Mavis and then go home and secure her doors and windows. Doctor Jerome was also reminded to be diligent and to watch for Martha who had threatened him shortly after she found out why Lila had entered Hillside. Doctor Jerome lived just a quarter mile from Hillside and his home was quite isolated. During the search, several other constables from the surrounding area were called in to cover the vast landscape that surrounded the town. The adoptive parents of Martha's baby were also temporarily moved into a safer location, fearing Martha may try and find her newborn son. Hysteria had now returned to Elmvale and it didn't take long before sightings were reported as far away as York.

Lila tried to go about her business, but she was constantly looking over her shoulder. Martha had been missing for almost forty-eight hours and no one had any idea where she was or how she was surviving in the extremely cold weather that had a grip on Northern Ontario. By all accounts she'd left wearing only a hospital gown, no stockings or shoes.

Detective Broad was certain she would die from exposure but until her body was found he didn't feel safe. On the afternoon of the third day, a candlelight vigil for Doctor Shield was held at St. John's Methodist Church on Main Street directly across from the Cannington Care Asylum. A crowd of over three hundred people who had been touched by the doctor attended. Prior to securing a job at the asylum, Doctor Shield was a family practitioner who took very good care of his patients. His kind and caring bedside manner would be very difficult to replace. Constable Blake and Detective Broad also attended and although they had never met the doctor, they were worried that Martha may show up and follow through on the threats she made to many of the nursing staff.

As more and more folks reported sightings of her, Martha would turn neighbour against neighbour. Rumours had spread among the locals as to why she hadn't been caught. No one believed that she could possibly survive outside in the frigid temperatures and some were sure that she was being sheltered by one of their neighbours.

The detective had never seen his town like this, and he didn't like what he was seeing. Fear had gripped Elmvale and until Martha Richards was caught and returned to the asylum, it would continue. Lila would only leave her home when she had a delivery and even this made her feel vulnerable.

Almost seventy-two hours after her escape, Detective Broad got his first bit of reliable information. Elmer and Trudy Carr had seen someone lurking around their barn. Elmer told his wife to stay back as he went out to see who it was but when he got to the barn, he found that whoever had been there had stolen his horse and a blanket. They didn't see her face but did say that the thief was of small stature and wearing only a white nightdress. Footprints in the snow were those of a woman, and droplets of blood were also found where the horse had been tied up. The couple's farm was only four miles from Elmvale and now the detective was worried that Martha was heading straight into town, to exact her revenge. Although Billy had heard about the theft at the Carr farm, he kept the news to himself. He knew if he printed it, panic would take over the entire town of Elmvale.

During this time the detective hardly slept. Keeping his town safe was his priority, and he wasn't going to allow Martha to get away with another senseless murder. The number of constables in town had tripled since her escape and he felt they were doing everything they could to make sure people were safe.

The news about Martha's escape reached London, Ontario, and Loraine was in touch with Lila almost daily. Feeling that she would be one of Martha's first targets, she pleaded with her to bring Isabel and join them in London. She felt that Lila would be safer having a greater distance between her and that lunatic. Lila declined her offer, but she certainly understood her concern.

A town hall meeting was called the following evening, inviting everyone wishing to voice their concerns to join the detective in a question and answer meeting. He was tired of chasing down false sightings and he needed to emphasize this. Time away from following real clues was his priority and crucial to finding this killer. Some of the rumours were utterly ridiculous, some said Martha Richards had begun dressing as a man, while others said she was a devil worshipper looking for her next offering.

Detective Broad, Constable Blake and psychiatrist Brent Taylor from the Cannington Care Asylum were there to take any questions pertaining to Martha Richards. Everyone that attended that night insisted they be told the real reason why she didn't hang for her crimes. Very few understood psychiatric illnesses and even when Doctor Taylor tried to explain, he received a collective booing followed by name-calling. Detective

Broad finally insisted they take one question at a time, and those that didn't adhere to the rules would be thrown out of the meeting. Finally, after two people were escorted out, the others settled down and order returned to the town hall.

During the meeting no one had any idea that Martha Richards was only a few hundred feet away. She had broken into the mercantile and stolen clothing, two butcher's knives and food items. In her haste she had dropped the remaining opium she had taken from the infirmary beside the door. Blood droplets were also visible in the newly fallen snow leading up to the mercantile. It appeared that Martha had tried to open the cash register but failed, as it was found upside down on the floor. Detective Broad was informed of these findings just after the town meeting ended. Officers patrolling the area had not seen her enter and they were just as baffled as he was as to how she had entered unnoticed.

When the detective asked Doctor Jerome about all the blood that was found in and around the mercantile, he said, "I can't give you an informative answer without seeing Doctor Shield's notes, but I believe she could be haemorrhaging now and frankly, I don't understand how this young woman is still alive. If she continues to lose this amount of blood each day, she will not survive much longer."

Considering her weakened state, the detective was shocked that she had any strength left at all. Still, he couldn't underestimate Martha's fierce determination to exact some sort of revenge on the people she perceived as her enemies.

Hoping to get a second opinion about the blood left in the mercantile, the detective asked someone that he knew was familiar with complications after childbirth and Lila came by to have a look inside. One look and Lila had to agree with Doctor Jerome, Martha was haemorrhaging. Lila had only seen this amount of blood when her mother delivered a baby after the mom had laboured for over forty hours, but her husband had failed to get help sooner. Now she was certain that Martha was in trouble and would soon collapse from the excessive bleeding. No one knew for sure how much longer Martha would survive but despite a heavy police presence in the area, she continued to elude capture.

20

All efforts to find Martha Richards that night failed, and it was now the morning of the sixth day since she escaped from Cannington Care Asylum. Everyone for miles around kept a close eye on their properties, but there had been no further sightings. Detective Broad assumed she had died and that they would not discover her body until the spring thaw.

Billy Carter also wrote an article that reflected the detective's thoughts. Lila wasn't convinced, she knew how determined Martha could be and despite her excessive blood loss, she was sure she would find the strength to exact her revenge on at least one of the people she had threatened in the past. Now feeling that she would be the target of her revenge, Lila had Isaac take Isabel to Elise's home until she felt it would be safe to bring her back. With Isaac working twelve hours a day in town, Lila was beginning to feel powerless, just as she had felt when Martha had left her on the floor that day with a broken leg.

Over the next two days, she sat by her window with Isaac's loaded hunting rifle on her knee and when the morning of the seventh day of Martha's escape arrived, the Elmvale Constabulary called off the search, which made Lila even more anxious.

Neither the doctors nor Detective Broad thought she was still alive and with this, the detective picked up his wife and children and brought them back home. Mr. Baines and the psychiatrists at Cannington Care Asylum felt the same way and contacted the detective to say they were closing her file and that her room would be occupied with another patient within the week.

The morning of February 2, 1908, a snowstorm began and didn't let up all day. By that evening there wasn't a soul seen in town and most of the shopkeepers had closed their doors and gone home. The storm was one of the worst the area had seen in years and only the essential services were in operation. By February 3, the weather had made travel impossible as the snow squalls were so blinding that nobody was safe to travel. After a lengthy discussion with his wife about staying home that day, Detective Broad rang the precinct to let Constable Blake know he wouldn't be in. This was highly unusual as he rarely took time off, but his wife insisted that he stay home and since there was nothing pressing to take care of at the constabulary, he agreed. The roads were nearly impossible to navigate and the ones that did venture out found themselves in ditches or stuck at the side of the road.

Although having a day off was unusual for Detective Broad, he was thoroughly enjoying it and managed to get some of the long list of chores done that he had been avoiding. After a nice dinner with his family, they sat by the fireplace and talked about their plans to visit his mother and father in Liverpool the spring of that same year. A few hours later, Sarah retired for the night, leaving her husband to tend to the fire.

Detective Broad sat quietly beside the fire, feeling about as relaxed as one could get. A little while later the glass of whiskey he was sipping dropped from his hand and fell on the carpet below. He had dozed off to sleep and was in the middle of a great dream about sailing when his wife came down to see why he hadn't come to bed. Sarah could see that he was sound asleep and not wanting to disturb him, she added wood to the fire, covered him with a woollen blanket and returned to bed. He would remain there until almost midnight when he awoke to the sound of his horses making a fuss in their nearby barn. As he peered out the window, he couldn't see the barn or anything else as a huge snow drift had covered much of it. A few seconds later he caught a glimpse of something moving around in the distance but he thought it was just a raccoon and quickly put it out of his mind. Knowing the horses were safely locked inside the barn, he made his way upstairs and joined his wife. Ten minutes later he got up again when he heard the horses moving about frantically. Detective Broad could clearly hear them thrashing around inside the barn as if something had found its way in. Now worried about the coyotes that had attacked his chickens last year, he decided it was time to have a look. After he got dressed, he took his rifle from the locked case and made his way to the barn. If it was a coyote causing all these problems he wanted to be prepared. Coyotes could be very dangerous if provoked and he wasn't taking any chances.

As he struggled to get through the snow and got closer to the barn, he noticed that the strong winds had opened the stall doors and snow had practically filled the entire area. After shovelling out the stalls and covering each horse with an extra blanket, they finally settled down. With only a dim light from the moon, he walked back toward his home and noticed fresh blood droplets leading away from the barn. His first thought was that an animal had been injured and that he would probably be finding the critter's body in the spring thaw. It wasn't until he saw more blood near the back door of his home that his thoughts changed, and fear of whom it was lurking nearby terrified him.

His heart was pounding as he tried to run back, but the heavy snow beneath his feet caused him to fall several times. With his rifle by his side, he crept upstairs and found that his wife and children were safe in their beds. If Martha was nearby, she hadn't attempted to get inside his home. Detective Broad stood at the back door, watching and listening for any unusual sounds, but the howling wind made it impossible to hear much of anything.

A few minutes later he noticed a shadowy figure lurking a few feet away. By now, his hands were so cold, he could barely hold his rifle erect and when he put his rifle down just for a few seconds to take his gloves from his pocket, he felt an excruciating pain radiating down his arm and into his chest. Martha had plunged the surgical knife she had stolen from the asylum deep into his back. As he fell forward into the snow, she lunged at him again, but this time she missed. His rifle was still by his side and although he felt himself passing out, he wasn't ready to die and with all the strength he had left in his body, he reached for the rifle and fired off two shots. Thankfully, one of the bullets hit its target and went into her chest. Martha, now dying, lay just a few feet from the detective.

By this time Sarah had heard the gunshots and came running down the stairs. Wearing only her nightdress, she ran to her husband's side and knelt down beside him. A neighbour had heard the gunshots too and had already called the constabulary. Although the weather was still making the journey treacherous, they managed to get there within fifteen minutes.

Upon arrival an ambulance was called and although Detective Broad was still alive, his condition was critical. Sarah, who was now covered in her husband's blood, was also taken to the hospital, suffering from hysteria. Detective Broad would be rushed into surgery that same night and his chances of survival were very slim. When Constable Blake secured the area, he saw that Martha was still laying in the snow that was now bright red. She was dead, but her cold, blue eyes stared up at him as if to say, "It's not over."

Back at the morgue the coroner determined that Martha Richards had died as a direct cause of being shot in her heart. He then removed Martha Richards' brain as requested by the head psychiatrist at Cannington. He studied the brains of the criminally insane, looking for any tell-tale sign that might cause someone to become a true psychopath. Martha's brain wouldn't reveal any secrets, but it was kept in jar of formaldehyde along with three others that had been diagnosed with the same affliction. Further testing would be done, several years later.

The rest of Martha's body was held in cold storage until the spring. She would eventually be buried in an unmarked grave just outside of town. News of Martha's death spread quickly throughout the town but no one celebrated as they awaited news of Detective Broad's condition.

The next morning, Detective Broad opened his eyes and looked around. Sarah was asleep in the chair beside his bed but his eyes wouldn't focus and at first, he thought it was Martha. Unable to speak loudly enough for anyone to hear him, he tried to reach for the bell to summon a nurse, causing him to fall out of bed. This woke Sarah who ran into the hallway screaming for help. Within minutes, Detective Broad was back in bed, realizing now that the woman in the chair had been his wife and not Martha Richards.

~

Back in Elmvale, the blizzard that had left its residents locked inside for days had now subsided, and with the news of Martha's death they began to venture outdoors again. Lila was able to get to the hospital to visit Detective Broad and was happy to see that he was on the mend and was going to make a full recovery.

Knowing that Martha Richards was dead was such a relief that Lila was finally able to get the rest she needed. Now five months pregnant and still very busy looking after Isabel and delivering babies, she was ready to put all of this behind her. Isaac had secured a very well-paid job at the Collingwood Academic College teaching sociology, and their futures were beginning to look very bright.

Everything seemed to be back to normal until she stopped in to see Billy on her way home that day. After purchasing a child's toy at the mercantile, Lila headed over to the *Examiner* only to find that its doors were locked. This was very odd as the last time she had spoken to Billy he had mentioned writing a book about Hillside Asylum and he asked that she come by to check over his first draft.

Lila was curious about this book but Billy wouldn't share anything, insisting she had to read it and then let him know what she thought. Now feeling that he had just left early that day, she headed back to Elise's home to pick up Isabel. It was as she went by her old house that a feeling of dread came over her. Billy was so punctual that she could set a clock by him. He never missed a day of work and now that she was thinking more clearly, she realized that she hadn't seen any of the *Examiner*'s papers recently. Surely he had heard about what had happened to Detective Broad and Martha Richards? Lila stopped for a moment and looked up at the window where her bedroom used to be. The urge to go back into town immediately came over her and instead of heading to Billy's home alone, she wisely went into the constabulary and spoke to Constable Blake about her concerns. If her hunch was wrong, she knew Billy would have a good laugh and Lila prayed that this would be the case.

Billy's house stood out among the rest in this posh neighbourhood as several flags from his native Scotland adorned the pathway leading to his front door. According to the neighbours, Billy hadn't been seen in days. A quick look inside the large bay window didn't reveal anything unusual, but the minute the officer stepped inside his home he knew that something was terribly wrong. The smell of death hung in the air like a heavy blanket and even with his scarf over his mouth, the constable could feel his stomach turning.

Lila had to turn around and go out as her pregnancy was already causing severe nausea. As she leaned up against the railing of his porch, she knew that the kindest and most thoughtful man she had ever had the pleasure of knowing was gone.

Lila never went back inside his home that day and thankfully she didn't see what Martha had done to him. Billy had over seventy stab wounds to his body, some inflicted after he had died. Pinned to his jacket pocket, the constable found an excerpt from an article he had written about Martha. It read: *A psychopath we all knew by the name of Margaret Reid has been found criminally insane and sentenced to life inside the Cannington Care Asylum. This punishment does not reflect what I would have chosen. Personally, seeing her swing by her scrawny little neck in front of hundreds of cheering onlookers would have been much more satisfying, but I digress, this I'm afraid, is as good as it's ever going to get, folks.*

In the end, Lila did read Billy's incredibly powerful manuscript and with the help of her best friend, she was able to publish it. It was accurately named *An Asylum Run by a Lunatic: The true story of what went on behind the doors of the notorious Hillside Asylum.*

The End

ACKNOWLEDGEMENTS

I would like to acknowledge my wonderful husband, Chris, for having the patience to listen to my stories, some of which I change numerous times before I am satisfied with the outcome.

I would also like to acknowledge my beautiful daughter, Kristin, who has not only supported me throughout this journey, but has been there when I am having a meltdown over a computer issue.

A special thank you to my sister, Susan; her strength, has also encouraged me to continue.

Last but certainly not least, are my two closest friends, Kim and Sandy. They have been by my side for many years, through good times and bad, and for this I am forever grateful.

A huge thanks to all of you!